D0544647

iRE

FRASER'S VOICES

NORTH EAST LINCOLNSHIRE
LIBRARIES

WITHDRAWN
FROM STOCK

AUTHORISED:

FRASER'S
VOICES

NORTH EAST	
LINCOLNSHIRE COUNCIL	
01026810	
Bertrams	05/04/2013
	£8.00

Jack Hastie

Copyright © 2013 C Jack Hastie

The moral right of the author has been asserted.

Apart from any fair dealing for the purposes of research or private study,
or criticism or review, as permitted under the Copyright, Designs and Patents
Act 1988, this publication may only be reproduced, stored or transmitted, in
any form or by any means, with the prior permission in writing of the
publishers, or in the case of reprographic reproduction in accordance with
the terms of licences issued by the Copyright Licensing Agency. Enquiries
concerning reproduction outside those terms should be sent to the publishers.

Matador
9 Priory Business Park,
Wistow Road, Kibworth Beauchamp,
Leicestershire. LE8 0RX
Tel: (+44) 116 279 2299
Fax: (+44) 116 279 2277
Email: books@troubador.co.uk
Web: www.troubador.co.uk/matador

ISBN 978 1780884 141

British Library Cataloguing in Publication Data.
A catalogue record for this book is available from the British Library.

Map, by Mary Hastie

Cover design by Mandy Sinclair

www.mandysinclair.com

Typeset by Troubador Publishing Ltd, Leicester, UK
Printed and bound in the UK by TJ International, Padstow, Cornwall

Matador is an imprint of Troubador Publishing Ltd

This book is dedicated to Amber, Erin, Mark and Courtney, the author's grandchildren.

CONTENTS

MAP OF THE AREA

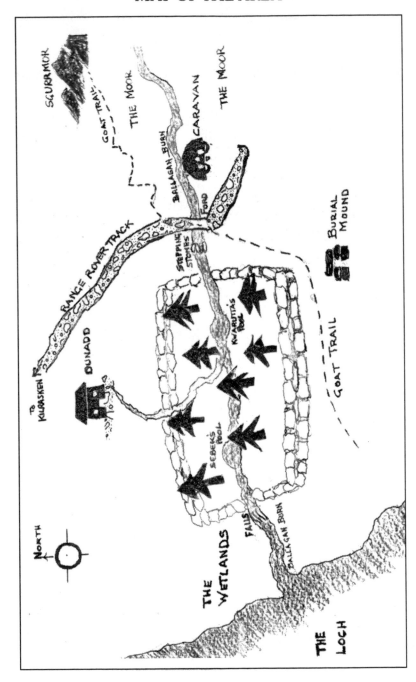

THE ASSASSIN

THE GIFT OF TONGUES

Fraser did not realise at first that something unusual had happened; he could understand the speech of birds.

On the window ledge beside his bed they perched, starlings and jackdaws, tiny sparrows and blue tits and occasionally huge seagulls blown inland by gales, and he understood what they were saying. Then he was discharged from hospital and taken to the cottage to recover.

"We don't really know what the trouble is," a doctor told his dad. "Keep an eye on him and let us know if there is any recurrence."

He would lie awake at night, afraid of those tumblings of the mind, worrying about what might be the matter with him and he would hear the shrill conversations of mice in the room and outside the whispering voices of bats, the calls of owls and sometimes, far away, the sharp bark of a fox.

Slowly he began to feel as if he had found a whole new family of friends on Facebook.

At first, although he understood most of the words, Fraser found it difficult to make much sense of what the birds and animals were saying. They talked so much about smells and sounds, flying or burrowing, building nests and hatching eggs, hibernating or migrating, that the conversations on which he eavesdropped were rather like those of his dad and his friends about politics and business, banks and investments, stocks and shares.

But gradually, as he picked up the language and came to understand a little of what it all meant, he began to appreciate some of the problems and hopes and fears of the speakers: the worry of a pair of starlings nesting under the eaves, with newly-hatched chicks, that Lucky, the black and white cat from across the road, who moved like a shadow and could climb almost as well as they could fly, might reach the nest; the grunted complaint of a bad tempered hedgehog about the shortage of fat black slugs in the garden; the twittering of two mice working up their courage to dart out into the middle of the bedroom for a crumb.

It was then that Fraser discovered that he could talk as well as listen.

The first time he tried it was by accident. A young male magpie, in his first mating season, had whistled a boast so outrageous – about fighting a sparrow hawk – to a hen, that, without thinking, Fraser found himself whistling in the language of the birds, "Believe that and you'll believe anything."

His lips had scarcely come back to their normal shape for human speech when he realised what he had done. The bird stood, beak agape, eyes wide with amazement, as if he could not believe his ears while the hen stopped preening herself abruptly, uttered a cackle of laughter and flapped off to another branch where a more mature male was practising his courtship patter.

Keen to experiment, Fraser tried out his new talent on someone else. A blackbird looked startled when he greeted it and flew to the safety of a higher branch, but then returned his compliment.

Starlings gossiped and argued so constantly among themselves that they accepted his contribution to their chatter and answered it without really noticing that it came from a ten year old boy and not from one of themselves. One of them even asked his opinion about the flavour of the beetles in the field on the other side of the garden wall.

At first Fraser found all this very interesting and he dreaded the day when his parents would announce that he was well enough to go back to school in Glasgow, away from his new friends. But after a while the novelty wore off. After all, catching beetles in a field isn't particularly exciting. Besides, Fraser was sure that no one would believe in his new gift and so, rather than be laughed at, he kept it all to himself – and he had nobody to share his adventures with.

Then came the mass murder.

Two doors away the people with the big garden kept hens. These lived in a run enclosed with wire mesh and slept at night in a big wooden coop. One night they were all slaughtered; fourteen hens with their heads bitten off and not one of them eaten.

Their owner swore vengeance on the killer, whoever he might be, and talked to a local gamekeeper about setting traps, putting down poison and sending out shotgun parties with assorted mongrels to drive the creatures of the woods and fields on to the guns.

At once the slaughter of the hens became the talk of the gardens. Fraser knew that some animals have to kill in order to live, but even the owl who night after night took a toll of mice and voles, and the gulls and rooks who thought nothing of taking live chicks from the nests of smaller birds, were horrified at the idea of such wholesale slaughter. Fraser learned too that even the boldest and most cunning of killers, the wildcat and the fox, shrank from taking farmyard animals, like ducks or hens or young lambs, because they knew that men would surely come with dogs and guns and traps and poisons and everyone would suffer.

As he idly kicked a stone by the side of a fence in the twilight one evening, Fraser listened as the birds voiced their suspicions as to who the murderer could be.

"Weasels, probably," said a jackdaw. "They always spoil things for themselves. Too greedy!"

"No weasel did that," answered an old rook. "Whoever did that dug right under the fence and then clawed his way into a corner of the coop where the wood was rotten. Reckon they'll be blaming One-eye."

One-eye, Fraser had heard, was the old fox, scarred victim and survivor of a hundred traps and fights and close encounters with dogs. Possibly, in his old age he might have taken to killing poultry, but why so many? Most of the birds felt that, like the cunning old dog he was, he would have taken what he needed and slipped away.

"He'll get the blame anyway," insisted the rook. "You watch. They'll be into all his earths with terriers in a day or two."

EYE OF THE WIND

Fraser had a strong sense of justice. Occasionally, at school he or one of his friends had been punished for something he had not done, and he had resented it. So the killer, if it really wasn't One-eye, would have to be found so that the fox wasn't chased out of his earth and trapped or shot for a crime he had not committed.

But if not One-eye, who else?

Fraser was only beginning to get to know the creatures of the woods and he knew that there must be many he knew nothing at all about, so he decided to try out his new tongue and see what he could discover.

One evening, a little before dusk, he walked deep among the trees and addressed a question to no one in particular.

"Who killed all the hens in the coop in the big garden?"

All at once there was silence, just like when the shadow of a hawk or an eagle falls on a field and everyone crouches down still and tries to hide. Fraser repeated his question and this time a particularly cheeky starling broke the silence.

"How should we know? None of our business."

"Then who does know?" persisted Fraser.

This time a magpie chirped up, "Go and ask Eye of the Wind. He sees everything," and he repeated the starling's remark, "None of our business."

Suddenly all the bird chatter broke out again as if they had all dismissed the thought of the killing from their minds.

"Eye of the Wind," wondered Fraser. He would have to ask someone who that was. "No use asking the birds," he muttered to himself. "They're too empty-headed to talk seriously about anything."

By this time he was almost through the wood and was just about to clamber over the dry stone dyke that marked its upper boundary, onto the open moor, when there was a hiss of wings, a crashing of curved talons, and a huge feathered thing skidded into a peat hag and bounced off again in disgust as a young rabbit dived, just in time, under the roots of a fallen tree.

Fraser caught a quick glimpse of a cruel eye and savagely hooked beak before the thing was off on the beating of powerful wings and soon no more than a speck in the sky.

"Ah!" gasped the rabbit, shaking himself to make sure he was really still in one piece. "Must be more careful. One chance too many, they say."

"That was close," said Fraser in the dialect he had learned from the mice in the cottage. "What was it?"

The rabbit looked up in amazement. What was this enormous creature that looked like a human boy and yet spoke like a fellow rodent and burrower? He retreated as far as possible under his root before replying.

"You mean you've never seen him before? You're lucky! But then you're too big for him; you don't have to worry."

"Maybe there are bigger ones who would come for me. Who is he? Where did he come from?"

"We call him Eye of the Wind because he comes out of the sky, from behind the sun. Nobody knows where he lives, but I did hear from a grouse that he has a nest somewhere up in the mountains."

Feeling that he had taken enough chances already that evening the youngster scuttled off into the deep cover of some heather and was lost.

Fraser looked up towards the blue hills that rolled endlessly along the horizon, broken only by the sharp crags of Sgurr Mor which jutted forward like the prow of a ship. Between the Sgurr and the wood lay the moor. He had never been close to it before and now, looking at it for the first time, he felt a sudden clutch of fear as he saw the terrible desolation of black peat hags, brown pools and grey rocks.

High above, somewhere, was Eye of the Wind, wheeling and circling, always circling.

Fraser felt completely helpless. He had never been in such a huge, empty place before. To track down Eye of the Wind in that wilderness must be impossible.

It was Klamath, the heron, who himself regularly flies over the moor from one fishing pool to another, who gave him some hope.

"Eye of the Wind is the golden eagle and he has a nest just like the rest of us. Up there," Klamath pointed with his long beak to the black cliffs which encircled the bald summit of Sgurr Mor. "A sheep track leads to the foot of the cliffs. If you can get up from there you'll find his mate sitting on eggs somewhere on a ledge. But take care. The only creatures who come anywhere near his nest are thieves, ravens and sometimes gulls; so if he sees you getting too close – and he sees everything – he'll try to knock you off your perch."

It was several weeks before Fraser could go. Day after day grey cloud raced across the moor wrapping the cliffs in a shroud of soaking cotton wool. And day after day Fraser turned away from his window to plan other adventures. Then, one day, a clean wind swept the sky, the moor bristled and the cliffs stood out, cracked and creviced, every ledge outlined by the slanting sunlight.

Fraser crept away, as he had planned, telling no-one, and set out to reach the crag-perched eyrie of the most dreaded predator on the moor.

The trail through the heather led gradually upwards towards the cliffs. From time to time he met grouse who exploded with a "Watch out! Watch out!" from almost under his feet, or a bolting hare, with bulging eyes that could see in all directions. Fraser tried to ask them about his search but, although they must have known about Eye of the Wind they were too startled, too quick to bolt, to stop and talk to him. Only a curlew, stepping delicately through the brown moor grass, told him, "Go home, boy with the bird's tongue. The cliffs are death to those who cannot fly."

So, under the hot sun, Fraser toiled upwards until he had left the grouse and the hares behind and stood at the foot of the cliffs, looking up. All he could see were towering columns split by a maze of cracks and crannies; the ledges where a bird might nest could not be seen from below.

What should he do now?

Just as he wondered there was a hiss of wings and a huge bird landed on a boulder a few yards away, balanced for a second and then folded his wings and eyed him. Fraser noticed the sharp, curved talons gripping the rock.

"What moves?" Fraser asked, using a phrase he had heard from a kestrel.

"Boy with a bird's tongue," came the reply in a harsh metallic voice. "Why have you come here?"

The giant bird flapped his wings several times and fluffed out his feathers. Fraser was afraid. His eyes kept coming back to those talons and that beak. "Who killed all the hens in the garden in the village?" he stammered. "They're blaming One-eye and… " Fraser started to explain his question, but the eagle cut him short with a clatter of his beak.

"How should I know that?"

"They say you see everything."

"I do, by day. I see everything that moves on land and in the air. But I do not hunt by night and even I can't see what moves under water. Go and ask Nephesh the owl."

DARK NIGHT; DEEP POOL

Nephesh was easier to find. He hunted around the gardens by night and Fraser could often hear him from his bedroom window.

That night he called to him. "Nephesh."

"What moves?" asked the owl, backing his wings and turning in flight to see who was calling him.

"Who killed all those hens?"

"Who asks?" The owl was suspicious and circled the house, peering with his enormous eyes.

"Here I am, at the window. I can speak your language."

"Ah! So it's true. I had heard from the bats, and Hobdax, the hedgehog had some second-hand tale to tell, but I did not believe that it was true. So you speak our language?"

"Who killed the hens?" repeated Fraser.

"Why should I know that?"

"Everyone says that you know all that happens by night," flattered Fraser.

The bird circled once more and perched on a chimney pot. He was pleased by the compliment and fluffed out his feathers with pride.

"Yes," he put his head to one side, "that is true. I hear most things that move in the night and whatever can be seen I see." Fraser tensed in expectation, his fingers gripping the windowsill. "But I do not know who killed the hens."

"I thought you knew everything." Fraser risked being cheeky.

"I do; I do," hooted the owl indignantly, "but this thing travels by water. He came down the burn that runs by the edge of the garden and he escaped the same way back into the wood, so that men and dogs could not track him. Am I a duck that I should see underwater?"

"An otter?" suggested Fraser.

"Definitely not an otter. No otter would kill like that. It was no animal I know of. Ask Sebek the Pike."

Fraser had to start all over again.

"Pike? Not worth catching," said a local angler. "Not much fight, no taste, nasty brutes. But if you really want to find a big one... " he directed Fraser to a deep pool in the Ballagan Burn down at the bottom of the wood and just above the rocky outcrop where it takes its last wild leap into space before flowing tamely into the loch.

Here, he was told, lived the great-grandfather of all the pike in Argyll. "Mind you don't fall in. He's as big as a crocodile, that one."

The pike was there, right enough. When Fraser lay on his side at the edge of the pool he could just see the silvery glint of the monster's scales through the dark brown, peaty water. But how to talk to him? It had never, until that moment, occurred to Fraser that fish could talk. But then he hadn't known that birds could either.

Eventually he asked a moorhen. After the usual startled flapping which was always the response when he spoke to a bird he hadn't met before, she settled down in the safety of a thicket of reeds and told him, "You'll have to shout. They're very deaf, fish. But he probably won't answer you anyway. He's also very rude... unless," she added as an afterthought, "you promise him worms; he's very greedy."

This turned out to be good advice. At first when Fraser spoke to him, Sebek just buried himself deeper in the mud at the bottom of the pool, if he heard him at all.

But after lunch Fraser came back with some tit-bits – the thick fat from a pork chop, two lumps of mouldy cheese his mum had been going to throw out and several worms he had dug out of the garden.

This did the trick and slowly the great fish rose, four feet from nose to tail, eyes staring straight ahead, mouth slightly open, showing long thin teeth, like needles. The coots and moorhens retreated to a safe distance for, although Sebek is lazy and such a poor swimmer that he is a joke among the trout, he can launch himself with one thrust of his tail like a torpedo on an unwary fish or waterbird and once those backward pointing teeth have closed on anything they cannot release their grip.

Sebek gulped the fat and cheese greedily.

"What moves?" asked Fraser.

"Who calls?" The pike's voice sent shivers down Fraser's spine, like a heavy file rasping over rotten wood.

Sebek could not see things out of the water very well and he was wary.

"Who killed all the hens in the man's garden?" Fraser knew his question by heart now.

"Hens? What are hens? What is a garden? I never leave this pool."

Fraser realised his mistake. Sebek was no Eye of the Wind, or even Nephesh who saw and heard most things.

He tried again. "A strange animal has killed a lot of birds. Do you know who it is?"

"I have taken birds," reminisced the pike. "Coots, ducks."

"But this is an animal that comes out on land," insisted Fraser.

The slow, cold-blooded fish continued with his memories. He was not to be hurried. "Animals too, frogs and voles. And once a young puppy dog came to drink. He waded in too far and I took him. I remember a human like you howling on the bank."

"But this killer was an animal that can leave the water."

"It has not come here. I would have taken it if it had. I never leave this pool now. You will see that I am very large and cannot now pass the shallows upstream. Once, when I was smaller, I…"

Fraser cut in, "But surely other fish tell you what moves upstream?"

"They do sometimes, the trout and the perch, but they avoid me. Few of them care to spend the time of day with me in my pool."

Fraser had exhausted the supply of worms he had brought with him and Sebek, whose only interest in the conversation, apart from boasting about his past exploits, had been in the bait, sank slowly to the deep dark bottom, like a water-logged tree trunk beyond the range of Fraser's questions.

BAROOK THE BADGER

The pale glow in the west had faded and in the opposite sky a low, orange moon was still too dull to give much light. Suddenly One-eye was at the mouth of the earth, nose wriggling, tasting the air before cautiously stepping out of the mouth of the burrow. He paused there for a second, still near enough to twist and bolt back underground, but the signs were safe; no strange scents and only the call of Nephesh as he slipped among the branches, his luminous, magnifying eyes scanning the ground for the least twitch of whisker or tail which would betray a mouse or vole.

"What moves?" barked One-eye.

"Nothing moves," hooted Nephesh, meaning that all was well.

One-eye stepped delicately from the play area just beyond the mouth of the den where generations of his cubs had tumbled and scratched and learned the first tricks of hunting; then he was on an old trail, trodden by his father and by generations of foxes before him.

He followed it through the wood, down by the side of the field. By now the lemon moon, climbing higher, was beginning to cast shadows, but below the trees all was blackness and One-eye moved by scent. Here the main trail was criss-crossed by the tiny traffickings of the wood-folk; recently a vole had hurried across into the cover of dense grass; further along a shrew had caught a beetle and had left the indigestible debris – legs and hard wing cases – as evidence of the murder; much earlier – too long ago to be of interest – a rabbit had hopped across the trail and sat on its hind legs – the grass was flattened – to survey the open field beyond the shelter of the trees.

One-eye's nose and whiskers and tongue told him all this and his old fox's brain knew what it meant just as Fraser's dad could look at a jungle of figures on a computer print-out and interpret the world of business.

Suddenly One-eye stiffened. Here was something unexpected; not strange or hostile but simply too good to be true.

"Carrion," his nose told him and it was as tempting as the smell of bacon frying to a hungry man.

He tracked it down the trail, for that kind of smell carries a long way. Then he saw it, the haunch of a rabbit. It must have lain for a week or more, for little things with many legs were beginning to fasten on the flesh.

At close quarters the smell was intoxicating, almost overpowering – yet there was something strange about the way the carcass lay that alerted One-eye's suspicions. So he checked, sniffed, looked and looked again and saw, like a spider's web of gleaming grey metal, the cage around the bait. It didn't move; it had no smell. Had he been younger, or perhaps hungrier, One-eye would have ignored it and gone for the meat, but he had not become One-eye, the survivor, for nothing and, sensing something unnatural which he did not understand, he stepped aside and followed the old trail till it led him away from that tantalising smell and on to the mice and frogs and other small game which were his night's normal business.

The moon, now silver, clambered over the backs of clouds up into a black sky, casting cold light across the fields and into the chequered spaces between the shadows of trees in the wood. The old trail shone like a marble causeway until its outline was broken by the hatching and blotching of the woodland shadows.

Along it came, snuffling and panting, One-eye's fellow lodger in the earth, Barook the Badger. Slowly he came, short of sight, rooting like a pig, grubbing for worms.

One-eye, who prided himself on being a hunter and delighted in nothing more than the sudden explosive charge and the capture of a young rabbit or hare off guard, despised Barook as a plodding, dull-witted beast content to live on worms and slugs. But he respected him too, for those powerful jaws and long claws were One-eye's protection against the only enemy he had to fear underground. Barook wasn't very clever and had no taste when it came to feeding, but, face to face in a narrow passage he would tear to pieces any terrier foolhardy enough to trespass on his territory.

Barook, grovelling for small crawling things, plodded down the trail following One-eye's scent till he came to the place where the fox had stepped aside. To be fair to him, he might have wondered why One-eye had done this so abruptly, but by then the delicious smell of dead rabbit was engulfing him in wave after wonderful wave.

He could smell no threatening scents and there were no strange sounds and so, without noticing the tell-tale metal web, he went for the bait. As his teeth met in it he heard, behind him, the clang of a portcullis.

The moon turned to copper and slunk out of the sky, the shadows it cast fading in the first grey glimmering of the dawn. Then the creatures of the night knew the time had come to return to their lairs before day revealed their secrets to the hawks and the dogs – and man.

One-eye trotted back along the trail with a good enough night's work inside him till he came to the strange scaffolding and inside it, as if to confirm his doubts, Barook.

"What moves?" asked One-eye.

"This moves. This web. I can't get out."

"You're trapped," snapped the fox.

"How do I get out?"

"You don't. You wait there till they come for you."

"By the bones of dead badgers, I will not," swore Barook, for he knew something about traps and what happened to those who were caught alive in them; and he tore at the cage till the blood spurted from his mouth and the pads of his paws.

The fox watched without emotion. He knew that there often comes a time in an animal's life when it makes one fatal mistake and finds itself with a weasel at its throat or a hawk's talons in its sides and then there is nothing more to be done. It seemed to him that Barook's death was already clenched around him and that he must get away as quickly as possible.

So he was just about to turn down the trail again when he remembered something and stopped.

"Get me out!" raved Barook.

"Wait," said One-eye. "The other day I heard a strange tale from Eye of the Wind of a boy who speaks our language. If it is true, perhaps he could help." And he bounded into the dawn.

RELEASE

Fraser had been asleep. Neither the growing light nor the full-throated dawn chorus of all the birds in Argyll had wakened him for it was still too early for most humans to be about, but something else had disturbed him.

What could it have been?

Then he heard it again – a tap-tapping at his window. This was not unusual. Some of the larger birds, jackdaws for instance, tapped on the pane quite often, possibly for insects. But then he heard a voice.

"Boy with the bird's tongue, boy with the bird's tongue, can you hear me?"

Fraser was wide awake at once. It was the first time a bird had ever started a conversation with him.

"What moves?" he whispered.

"Put your head out of the window and listen."

Fraser got up, drew back the curtain and opened the window. Immediately a magpie flapped off to a tree and, settling in a low branch, spoke to something on the ground in the bushes.

"There he is."

There was little light yet and before Fraser could see anything in the shadows below the sycamores he heard a noise halfway between a whine and a growl; the animal seemed uneasy about speaking directly to a human inside a house.

"Is it true what Eye of the Wind said? Can you understand me?"

"Yes," said Fraser realising now that he was talking with a fox.

"Then follow me."

Never in his life had Fraser come across a story in which a fox called on a boy to follow him, or a boy followed a fox.

"But the animal was insistent. "Come. At once."

"I'm coming. Wait a moment; humans need clothes."

Pulse pounding, he pulled on jeans and a sweater, crammed his feet into a pair of trainers and slipped over the window sill on the trail of a wild creature that had asked him to follow it.

One-eye – Fraser could see now that the fox he was following was the one he had heard about and had been trying to help – trotted ahead, but stopped frequently to look back and make sure the boy was following. The trail led through a gap in the garden wall round the edge of a field and into the wood. Here One-eye seemed to feel that his mission had been completed, for he flattened his body to the ground, gave several sharp barks, "Here! Here!" and, clearly uneasy in the growing light of day, cantered off into the undergrowth...

Fraser looked about. It was not yet quite light under the trees.

Then he heard a gruff voice, "Can you get me out?" and saw the trap – a steel cage with a deadweight door released by pressure on a pad just in front of the bait. He'd often seen them before and one of the gamekeepers had shown him how they worked. Inside this one was a large badger bleeding from mouth and paws.

It never occurred to Fraser not to release the animal. He had been brought into the secret confidence of wild things and he could not have betrayed that confidence. Quickly he lifted the trapdoor and the badger scrambled out and vanished into the undergrowth. Fraser was somehow disappointed. What had he expected? That a frightened wild animal would sit up and give a paw, like a poodle, and say "Thank you"?

He turned and was just about to make his way home, hoping that he had not been missed from the house, when that rough voice called to him from the density of a bramble thicket where the animal felt safe.

"I owe you a debt. My people have long memories. One day I will repay."

Then, with a scuffling in the undergrowth, he was gone.

Fraser was not to know how soon he would have to count on that promise.

KILRASKEN FARM

The only person Fraser tried to tell about his gifts and his adventures was Jim Douglas, a boy a year older than himself who lived in Kilrasken Farm. They got on well, but when Fraser tried to explain about animal speech Jim just thought he was kidding.

"You talk to the birds! Aye, that'll be right. Listen, mate, I've lived on a farm all my life and I know all about the beasts. Don't try to take the mickey."

At first Fraser had been hurt, but Jim hadn't been unkind and had simply taken Fraser's confidences as a kind of joke. Besides, Jim was an interesting character; he really did know the ways of the animals, from the rats in the barn right up to the bad-tempered bull, who, he told Fraser, would charge and trample to death any stranger in his field but allowed himself to be driven like a tame sheep by Jim because Jim understood the ways of beasts.

So Fraser gave up.

That was just as well. Jim had been taught to disapprove of animals like foxes and badgers who sometimes took lambs and young birds, and the very idea of letting one of them out of a trap would have seemed to him like treachery to the human race, or at least to all farmers and gamekeepers.

The boys enjoyed exploring together and as Fraser's recovery progressed he would go up to the farm for days on end. Jim, the expert, delighted in showing the boy from the city all the secrets of the place.

The main attraction was the disused barn. There was an old tractor there, quietly rusting with a steering wheel that could still turn and a gear lever and pedals that moved. The dark corners of the barn were a wonder house for a pair of boys to play in; the sacks of poultry feed and piles of assorted rubbish – old tyres, parts of a plough, rusty horse shoes, a grinning gin for trapping foxes and birds of prey, ("You're not allowed to use that now," Jim explained), bits of bedsteads and bicycles, a ram's skull with the giant circling horns still attached.

Most exciting of all, when they came on a still evening and rushed in quickly, throwing everything about and shouting their personal war cries, they would hear scufflings and sometimes see the whiplash of a long grey tail as its owner dived for cover.

Rats," explained Jim. "All over the place. That's what we keep the dogs for." But Misty and Tess were always away in the fields working the sheep with Jim's dad, and Fraser had to take Jim's word for the prodigious rat killing powers of the two collies.

They got closer to the rats when they tiptoed quietly into the barn; then they would see them, with twitching noses and watchful eyes furtively poking among the rubbish. More often, even when they couldn't see them, they could hear the rats' squeaking calls.

Fraser, of course, could understand them;

"What moves?"

"Two humans. Be careful."

"No dogs?"

"Sssh! Keep still. The humans will call the dogs if they see us."

But there would have been no point in translating for Jim.

On other days they went further afield; Jim showed Fraser the lambing shed, built the year before within sight of the house so that his dad could bring sick ewes there to have their lambs where he could look after them more easily than if they had been born out in the fields where One-eye or Eye of the Wind might steal them. There were no ewes there now, but two lambs, whose mother had rejected them and who were being reared by hand, lay curled up against each other, like balls of creamy fluff in a bed of warm straw.

Then there was the dunghill where the manure of ages was slowly breaking down into compost, alive with worms. The boys weren't officially allowed to play there – they never could understand why – but as it was behind the lambing shed and the hen houses and out of sight of the farm house, they would sometimes go there and count how many worms they could catch. Then they would take their haul round to the duck pond to see if the ducks would eat them. But either the ducks were nervous, for they had half-grown ducklings with them, or they just didn't like worms, for they kept their distance. So the boys would squat by the edge of the pool and drop the worms in one by one to see if they could swim.

Here, however, they *could* be seen from the house and Jim's mum seemed to know where they got the worms from; so that adventure always ended with her calling, "Right boys. In you come and get cleaned up," in a voice that had to be obeyed.

* * *

Fraser was not the only newcomer to the area to discover Kilrasken.

One-eye and Barook knew better than to come near the place, but someone else with the courage of a badger, the cunning of a fox and a hatred of man had discovered a trail that ran out of the wood, along a hedgerow and up to the farm buildings. On its first foray it discovered the barn and for several nights feasted on rats.

But it hunted, not for food nor even for pleasure, but for revenge and so, on the fourth night, moonless and black as pitch, it pressed on, in full sight of the house, and found the lambing shed.

There were lights in the windows of the house but the curtains were drawn and the dogs were dozing by the fire.

The two lambs heard a soft scratching and were awake at once, scrambling onto wobbly legs. There, unseen in the darkness but its stink shaking the shed, was the demon nightmare of every small animal's imagination. Then the rattle of claws on the floor, the pant of hot breath, the clash of teeth and it was on them.

Perhaps Misty, the younger dog heard the brief, terrified bleat. Suddenly her ears were erect, the hair on her neck lifted and from deep in her throat came a low growl. Seconds later the ducks and hens took up the warning and the henhouse shook with a frenzied beating of wings, crowing and quacking.

Jim's dad threw a switch and the courtyard was flooded with light. Jim swept back the curtains and saw, leaving the lambing shed and vanishing into the shadows behind the barn, an animal like nothing he had seen before.

"It sort of looped," he said later, trying to recall for the benefit of his dad and the gamekeeper what he had seen only for a fraction of a second and out of the corner of his eye.

Naturally Jim added a little to the story when he told Fraser – the animal had got bigger – "like a wolf" – and he had to stick to this version when the man from the *Kilmore Gazette* came to get the story.

"Mystery killer at Kilrasken" the headline read and the paper went on to wonder what kind of monster had torn out the throats of the two young lambs.

Readers' letters in the following issue offered some suggestions:

One reader thought that "a giant flesh eating lizard of the monitor type, which can grow up to six feet in length," might have escaped from a private zoo. An elderly lady was sure it was the ghost of a witch who had been drowned in the loch three hundred years before; and a sixth former from the High School proposed that it was an alien from space connected with recent sightings of unidentified flying objects.

Fraser found most of this impossible to translate into the language of his friends. The birds had quickly brought the news from Kilrasken, but no one had any idea who the killer could be.

So Fraser decided to go back into the wood and find out for himself.

THE ROOKS

He was nearing the edge of the wood and the mist of branches was thinning out. The clouds broke and a dazzling low sun threw shafts of slanting light between the trees. Light and dark; light and dark; Fraser's mind began to beat to a rhythm as his eyes crossed and re-crossed the lines of light and shade, up and down, up and down. He remembered the last time in the car, at Easter in France – poplars – lines of tall trees like sentries and the brightest sun he had ever seen – light and dark flashing – flick, flick, flick, flick as the car raced on – flick, flick, flick, flick like a shutter clicking in his mind – then blackness – hospital and the bird language.

He was falling…

"Dead boy," remarked an old rook perched on a high branch directly above Fraser.

"Probably just sleeping," said another argumentatively with a clatter of his dirty beak.

"Think so?" said the first. "Well I saw the way he fell. He's dead all right."

"So what?" quarrelled the second, a younger bird who had not lived long enough to be quite sure of himself but felt he ought to appear knowledgeable. "We can't eat him till he's rotted a bit."

"Ever tried their eyes?" went on the first. "Don't even have to be right dead, so long as they can't move. Like picking beetles from a rose bed. And tastier! Tastiest bite I've had, come to think of it."

"You've picked out dead men's eyes?" cawed the younger bird in admiration.

"Not quite," admitted the older rook. "Not actually men. Done it often enough with sheep on their backs; they can't do a thing. Once with a young calf. Anyway, fancy this one? One each, eh?"

Like most rooks this veteran liked to boast and the pleasure of showing the youngster how to do it would be worth the other eye. Besides, the old boy knew it wasn't quite as easy as he had suggested and he wanted moral support.

The two flapped down to a low branch and then to the ground. There they walked – rooks are too conceited to hop – backwards and forwards as if interested in anything but the boy lying a few yards in front of them. They had to work up their courage. Anyway, the older one now realised that he had made a mistake; the boy was still breathing. Not that that made a lot of difference – but you had to look sharp – might only get one eye. If he had been alone he would have abandoned the plan and flown off, but with an admiring youngster watching and a reputation to keep up... so he strutted about ceremoniously trying to gather up his courage for the final rush, stab and quick take-off.

By now all the birds in the wood had realised what was going on. Few of them liked the rooks, who stole their eggs and chicks, and, although none of them would have taken any risks to help a human being, their sympathies were with the boy. Besides, it was now clear that the older rook was unsure of himself and that gave some of the cheekier birds the chance to make mischief.

"Scared! Scared! Scared! Scared!" shrieked a magpie, swooping low over the path.

"Want me to show you how?" chattered a jackdaw, who might, if the moment had been right, have been as good as his word.

"Chicken killer," moaned a pigeon who had lost two of her brood and suspected the rooks.

Immediately the smaller birds took up the cry. "Chick-en kill-er, chick-en kill-er," they chanted and flew in circles above the two rooks.

This only made the older bird more determined – the younger had retreated a few yards to a low branch – and he stepped purposefully towards the boy, beak darting forward and back at each stride.

In the fox's earth, just outside the wood, One-eye was sleeping lightly after the custom of his family. He turned in his sleep, awoke and scratched himself. It was midday and no time for hunting, but some sixth sense, to which foxes often owe their lives, made him amble up to the mouth of the den instead of simply curling up again and going back to sleep. There he heard the commotion in the trees.

"What moves?" he growled.

A confusion of a hundred voices answered him, "Boy dead! Rooks... eyes."

It made no sense, but foxes are curious and there is always a little empty space inside them for an unexpected tit-bit, so One-eye decided to investigate and stepped out of the tunnel. As soon as he saw the situation he realised that this was no hunting for him. Then he saw that the unconscious boy was Barook's rescuer. With a couple of sharp barks that put the two rooks to flight for the moment, he turned back to the lair.

Badgers do not wake up, let alone venture above ground by daylight, but when Barook was rooted out of a beautiful sleep by One-eye's wet black nose and told what was happening, he remembered his promise and, rumbling his warcry, "Barook, Ya-Barook, Ya-Barook," galloped out, blinking, into the hostile strange sunshine to honour his pledge.

Half an hour later Bob Paterson, who lived across the road from Fraser, was walking his labrador in the woods. He too heard the commotion of the birds and the dog ran on ahead. Moments later it was back, whining, tail between its legs, and, as Bob walked on, fell, uncharacteristically, behind his heel. Bob told his story that night.

"I saw the lad lying on the path and beside him, in broad daylight, a badger, every hair on its back bristling and every tooth bared."

Only when he had put his dog on the lead and gone over to look at the boy had the animal turned and vanished into the undergrowth.

RECOVERY

Fraser's adventure in the wood had one good result, from his point of view. It postponed for a time the day when he would be pronounced recovered and sent back to school in Glasgow. In fact it put him into the local hospital for a week for observation. As he didn't feel anything wrong he would have been bored out of his mind if it had not been for his conversations with the birds, and, although these were, as usual, surprised and suspicious at first, they soon got used to him and would even fly off and bring him news of what was happening beyond what he could see from the window of his ward.

Most of this didn't really interest him – a rook's story of a dead hedgehog in the hospital car park – the tale told by a big black-backed gull of a delivery of fish left unattended for a minute by the kitchen staff – the warnings of smaller birds of kestrels in the hospital gardens.

But he did hear something more interesting from a wild drake, a mallard who settled for the night in an ornamental pond in the grounds just outside the window.

The drake was exhausted and had clearly flown some distance.

"Decided to shift my quarters," he quacked. "Big party of men and dogs came through the woods just before dark. We weren't worried, my mate and I. We just got into the water. But then, from the other side, came more men with the tame lightning." (The mallard meant guns, but, as all birds and animals fear guns and none understands them, they make up all sorts of ways of describing them.)

"They were shooting at everything. The small animals went underground, so they shot the birds. My mate was killed; I was lucky."

"Why did they do that?" asked Fraser, who had never seen a shoot.

"Don't know. Some of the tree birds say there's been farm animals killed. The gamekeepers set a trap and it was raided. The bait was taken but nothing caught. That's the second reason I came away. My friends, the coots and moorhens, tell me there has been something coming out of the water by night. It attacks them in their nests. A lot of them have been killed. 'No place for me,' I said. 'Dogs and guns by day; something from the water by night; my mate dead; time to go.'"

Fraser's other important conversation was with someone called "the consultant" the day his dad came to take him back to the cottage.

This time the hospital people *did* seem to know what his trouble was. The consultant produced a flat cardboard box with "Keep out of reach of children" printed prominently on the side. He opened one end and slid out a strip of silver paper with the days of the week printed on it and below each day a large, round, brown pill stuck under cellophane.

"You'll remember to take one every day. You musn't ever miss a day."

Fraser nodded.

The consultant replaced the strip and handed the box to Fraser's dad.

"He should be all right now. He's stable, provided he takes one every day."

They went back to the cottage and in a week Fraser's parents said he was so much better that he could go to stay for a few days with Jim Douglas on the farm.

When he arrived Jim was there to meet him and the two dogs, Misty and Tess, came bounding out, barking a welcome. On his previous visits the dogs had always been out working the sheep with Jim's dad and this was the first time he had heard them talk.

By now Fraser was so used to understanding all the animal chatter that went on around him that he was surprised to discover that he could make out only a little of what the dogs were saying, as if he was listening on a crackly telephone line to someone with a foreign accent.

"That's funny," he thought. "Perhaps tame animals speak a different language."

KWARUTTA!

In the heart of the wood lay a tiny lochan threaded like a bead on the Ballagan Burn as it tumbled and splashed from the moors down through the wood and at last pushed its way through marshes and mudflats to enter the loch.

Once the lochan had held trout, and mallard and moorhen had nested by its edges, but it was empty now. Twenty yards from the bank, buried in ferns and brambles, sat the ruins of a cottage. The walls still stood shoulder-high, but long ago the roof and the higher parts of the gables had collapsed into a pile of stones and slates and rotten timbers, under which a hundred rats might have nested in safety. But there were none there now.

Slowly, from a crevice between two of the fallen stones, there emerged, first the muzzle, then the silky seal-like head and finally the sleek body of a full-grown mink.

He was not a native to these parts, having recently escaped from a farm in which he and his kind were bred and killed for their fur. His family came from Canada where he was proud to be cousin to the wolverine who could drive wolves from a kill.

He slipped into the pool and swam across, wasting no time, for long ago the other inhabitants had been killed by this cleverest and boldest of hunters. On the far side trails led off in two directions. One led to the farms and the village where the mink had been hunting for the last few nights, but here the scent was heavy with men and dogs for they had at last tracked him as far as this.

Tonight, therefore, he turned in the other direction and headed up towards the moor. This was a different world from the woods and farmlands. Here tracks of big blue mountain hare, of grouse, and of adders wound in the black peat among rocks and clumps of heather and fern and the droppings of sheep and red deer.

The smells were strong and exciting, and, after pausing for a moment to drink them in, he set off up the trail. He had not gone far when he was stopped by a new sound; a wild, unearthly cry from something higher up on the moor. The mink stiffened. The creature was down wind, so he got no whiff of its scent. By its call it was a predator like himself. If it was his size or smaller he would kill it. If it was larger he would still kill it. If it was so large as to be beyond his power he would find it easy to escape in this bristly country.

But his own strong scent rode ahead of him on the light wind and told the other hunter that a rival was intruding on his territory. The other animal took up the challenge, bounded down the trail and then froze, crouched on stiff legs, back arched, tail lashing; the mink found himself face to face with Cruach, the wild cat.

The two killers eyed each other.

"Get off my ground," spat the cat.

"Your ground? You will have to prove that. I hunt where I please." The mink's jaws shut like a trap on the words.

The cat hissed, "You're a stranger here. You've no right on my ground. Get off it or prepare to pay the price." His back was arching dangerously and, as he spoke, his lips curled back to show long, needle-like fangs bared back to the pink gums.

More dangerous still, as he raised a front paw to strike, it was suddenly armed with five curved scimitars, unblunted by the wear and tear of walking and running, for the cat alone can sheath and unsheath his claws like a forest of swords.

The mink was not intimidated.

"I did not choose to live in your wretched land," he replied. "My tribe comes from a better country far away, a country of rivers full of fish and woods full of game. But we were trapped and killed by man," he went on savagely. "So I was born in a cage and lived in a cage till one day I saw the wire loose in the wood, and I tore it away, remembering that I am Kwarutta, the hunter, and no pretty flower to dress a painted lady.

"And so I came here killing as I needed, killing as I wished. But most of all I kill to take my revenge on man and his slaves, his fat farmyard hens, his grouse on the moor, his cats and his dogs." The voice had risen to a hissing scream, "and, one day, when they are unguarded, even his young. Then will I kill and kill and kill until at last the blood debt of my tribe has been repaid."

This kind of talk was new to the cat. He could appreciate a slow careful stalk through thick grass, the sudden explosive charge and the satisfaction of teeth meeting in the throat of a victim, but this single-minded vendetta against the whole human race sent shivers down his spine.

"I have no liking for men," he replied, "but I have nothing to do with your war. Fight it in the farmyards and the gardens, but keep off my ground."

Neither animal now wished matters to come to a clash of teeth and claws. Like boys in a school playground who have squared up to each other and each stood his ground, they now respected each other and wanted to withdraw with honour.

"Between two such hunters as ourselves let there be peace," said Kwarutta. "I will hunt here no more. But when the gamekeeper has poisoned your litter and shot your mate for the sake of his grouse, join me one moonless night and together we will repay him in his henhouses."

He turned, and with the looping gait of his family, headed for the farms.

THE DAWN RAID

Jim took the greatest pleasure in telling Fraser about the mysterious killings that had led to the great shoot-out in the wood which the mallard had described: more hens; a pet rabbit in a garden hutch; young, hand-reared partridges in a gamekeeper's yard. Whoever it was, the killer seemed to take special pleasure in boldly entering sheds and coops and hutches close to human houses and killing, but rarely eating animals that were close to people.

It had been tracked with dogs but the trails had always led to water and the dogs had stopped, baffled by a burn or a pool in the woods. It had even – so Jim had heard – lifted bait from a trap which it had somehow sprung without being caught.

Fraser was anxious to ask the birds or even the cattle and sheep on the farm if they had heard anything more, but it was difficult with Jim around and somehow their voices seemed confused and far away. There was also the distraction of the barn – the tractor, the tyres, the bicycles and bedsteads, and the two boys made enough noise to frighten away the bird life for acres around, not to mention the rats.

Bedtime came and they slept by an attic window overlooking the farmhouse courtyard. Before he settled to sleep that long, bright May evening, Fraser took a last look at the lambing shed, now empty, the henhouses melting into the dusk and, away to his right, the dark surface of the duck pond with the white shapes of the farmyard ducks settling, heads twisted back, bills buried under the soft down of their backs, for the night.

When he wakened it was again half light and the dawn chorus of the birds was just beginning.

He looked out of the window and saw the same peaceful scene as the previous evening. Then he saw something else: like a hump-backed snake with short, clawed legs, chocolate brown in the grey brown of the dawn.

"Jim," he hissed.

The two boys' heads crammed the attic window.

The mink looped across the courtyard, its eyes on the ducks.

The boys watched, hypnotised.

Then the dawn exploded. A drake unburied its bill and quacked an alarm. The cry was taken up by the other ducks and by the hens in the coop.

The door of the house flew open, floodlight drenched the courtyard and Misty and Tess bounded out to seek and destroy. Kwarutta, full of hate, turned on the dogs and, leaping for Misty's muzzle, jumped almost into the jaws of Tess. Fraser heard the crack as the mink's skull collapsed under the vice of the collie's back teeth.

There were no more killings.

Fraser came back to the cottage, stayed there for another week and remembered to take his pills every day. The consultant said he was better and certainly he did not feel any of those frightening tumblings of the mind which had so disturbed him after he had first gone to hospital. And he had no more blackouts. So they said he had to go back to school in Glasgow.

Fraser didn't mind.

For when he went into the garden teeming with birds all he heard were whistles and chirrups, and in the wood the quarrelsome cawing of the rooks was – only cawing. Even the eloquent alarm cry of the blackbird, "Take care! Take care! Take care!" was only a trill.

At night, as he watched in sadness from his window, Nephesh the owl, who could, he knew, have told him where every vole and shrew was crouching in the long grass, said only "Whooo—oh."

Fraser tried the old call, "What moves?" but all that came was a sigh. And when he heard in the distance One-eye give the call that must have meant "What moves, Nephesh?" and all he could hear was "Aaargh!" he knew that it was over.

"Nothing moves," he said to himself in human speech. "Tomorrow I must listen to different voices."

Tears streamed down his cheeks.

THE CARAVAN

THE OTTER

The otter died.

Fraser had nursed it for a week. "Did everything he could," everybody said. Cathy, the vet, had said it might have swallowed some kind of poison, but, as she told Fraser, "Otters can't speak; so we don't really know what was wrong with it."

She had treated it with antibiotics, but hadn't held out much hope, and a few days later it had died.

Fraser was inconsolable. This was the first time he had thrown himself into caring for a sick animal, and it had died.

"You did all you could," repeated his mum.

But he was not convinced. So he asked Rona, the vet nurse, Cathy's assistant, "If Cathy had known what kind of poison the otter had eaten, could she have cured him?"

Rona was sixteen and had just started a college course about how to be a vet nurse, so Fraser was sure she would know. She was kind and gentle with sick and frightened animals. She could hold a struggling guinea pig till Cathy gave it an injection; she could persuade a big, silly labrador to stand still and have his temperature taken. She was kind with people too; she had understood how upset Fraser had been when the otter died.

"You mustn't blame yourself," she insisted.

Then she told him her secret; how once she had been to blame for an animal's death.

"I had just got a new puppy. I took him for a walk in the woods. I let him off the lead – I shouldn't – and he slipped

43

into a deep pool." Her eyes filled. "Something caught him and pulled him under the water."

Doggedly Fraser persisted with his question.

"Could Cathy have cured the otter?"

"Perhaps she could, but that's what it's always like with animals; they can't tell us what's wrong with them."

It was then that Fraser knew that he had let the otter down.

It was over a year since he had been ill and had first come to the cottage to recover. He was well and strong now and the year had been spent at school in Glasgow, playing football, watching television and playing computer games till his eyes almost popped out of their sockets, like a frog's.

But sometimes, in the quiet of his bedroom, he remembered his friends from the cottage; One-eye the fox; Nephesh the owl; the frightening eagle, Eye of the Wind.

There were animals and birds in Glasgow; street cats, dirty looking pigeons and thousands of starlings, but Fraser had lost the power to speak with them.

But there was always the football. So One-eye and the others got a passing thought from time to time, like old well-loved toys, now lost, while the main priority was football; training and tactics, and the chance to go to a big match on Saturday afternoons.

Then came the summer holidays and at the end of a hot, dry June he found himself back at the cottage; and the old memories returned. Still the world of animals was lost to him, almost like something he had read in a book or dreamed – till the otter died.

* * *

Jim Douglas was not sentimental about animals. How he had danced a triumphal dance and what a war song he had shrieked when his dog Tess had killed Kwarutta, the mink, the year before. During the past year Jim's dad had taken him fishing and shooting so that he now prided himself on how many animals he had killed. He kept a running tally of the number of rats the collies had killed in the barn and those that he had personally chased from their hiding places into the dogs' jaws he counted as his own kills.

Fraser found that he liked Jim less this year, but the farm was still a good place to play and Jim, for all his outward contempt for the animals, was still full of interesting stories about them and their ways.

It was from Jim that Fraser learned about the dead fish in the Ballagan Burn. Rona contributed some more information about wild ducks sick and unable to fly. She agreed with Fraser that there might be some mystery disease about, though Cathy thought not. But then Cathy spent most of her time looking after big animals like horses and cows and sheep and pigs, or toy animals like poodles or Siamese cats that were never allowed out.

Fraser decided that Cathy didn't really understand the situation and that he would have to help Rona to get to the bottom of the mystery. So, one night, before going to bed, he crept to the bathroom and, deliberately and ceremoniously, slid a strip of silver paper from a flat cardboard box, removed a round, brown pill – and dropped it into the toilet.

He stared guiltily as the flushing, gurgling water swept away his medicine. The consultant had said that he must *always* take one *every* day. He remembered the flashing lights and the tumblings of his mind. But, in his imagination, he also heard, across the still night air, the old call, "What moves?" and, more than anything else in the world, he longed to hear it again.

THE CARAVAN

The Range Rover's engine screamed as Archie thrust it into reverse gear and the four tyres spun and kicked up clods of brown clay, mixed with gravel as they clawed for purchase on the new track that sliced like an open wound, across the slope of the moor.

But Archie knew his job and, inch by inch, he backed the caravan into the narrow slot, little more than a ledge, which had been carved from the hillside to take it.

"OK. She'll do," shouted Dyer, and Archie slid the gear lever into neutral and put on the handbrake.

"That suit you then?"

"Yeah. Fine."

"Boss says you're to empty the toilet over there, in the peat. You'll have no bother burying it."

They uncoupled the van from the towing hook and put chocks against the wheels.

"Mind you," went on Archie, "if you get a real downpour that slope'll be awash and the whole site'll get swept away. Your van'll go over that crag and it won't stop till it hits the trees down there."

"No chance," said Dyer. "But anyway, I'll anchor the van and make sure it won't shift."

"Trust me, the site's not safe. Slope above's too steep, the way you've left it. The whole thing'll move if you get a bad spell of wet weather."

"Thanks for the tip," said Dyer and Archie put the vehicle into first gear and churned down the track the way he had come.

Peace.

Dyer surveyed his new home. For an artist he could hardly have chosen a more impressive spot. Behind him the black crags of Sgurr Mor reared menacingly and its peak almost seemed to overhang the caravan site, like a dinosaur frozen in stone, waiting, perhaps, to come alive and strike.

With just the hint of a shudder he turned away and looked straight ahead, down the hill. In front of him the moor tumbled steeply downwards for about two hundred feet till an ancient dry stone dyke stopped it like a dam, and beyond this lay the woods, and farmlands with the buildings of the clachan* of Dunadd huddled together like dolls' houses, and beyond that the loch shining, with the golden path of the setting sun burning across it.

On the far side of the loch three sharp blue peaks were silhouetted against the fiery red sky. "One of the islands," he thought. "Must check it out on the map."

There was such a lacework of lochs and islands, and lochs on islands, and islands in lochs that Dyer found the geography pretty confusing, and the fact that they all had quite unpronounceable Gaelic names didn't help. But he was sure he would learn enough of the language to make sense of it all – after all he'd had the same sort of problem with Aborigine names in the outback down under.

What he hadn't had to contend with was the West Highland weather, though at first that treated him so kindly that he simply couldn't believe the tales he had heard of torrential downpours and week after week of rain.

He turned to look at his nearer surroundings. The Range Rover Track had recently been cut by the new owner of the moor to replace an old pony trail so that the carcasses of stags could be taken down more easily in the stalking season.

*hamlet

It forded the Ballagan Burn and stopped at the caravan site, beyond which the ground rose steeply for about fifty feet and then the moor levelled off in a soggy morass of peat too treacherous even for ponies to negotiate. That was where he would have to bury the contents of the chemical toilet,

Even here there was a trail of *sorts*. It began low down in the bracken above the woods and crossed the new Range Rover Track at the very spot where the ledge had been cut in the hillside to take the caravan. But it continued beyond that, winding up the slope until it disappeared from sight on the moor. Along this trail and all round the caravan were the prints of cloven hooves, as if hundreds of animals had tracked backwards and forwards over the spot for centuries.

"Sheep? Deer? Haggis?" Dyer laughed at his own joke. "Have they really got legs on one side longer than the other?"

Dyer painted landscapes; sunsets and sunrises; coral islands drowsing in the heat. Animals didn't interest him.

Ayers Rock at sunrise had been breathtaking, but now he needed cloud effects; fleeces of mist half veiling the mountains; thunder clouds brooding over empty moors; sudden shafts of sunlight reflected from lonely lochans; the kind of lighting that could make you imagine ancient ghosts; kelpies – milk white horses peacefully grazing by the shore of a loch who would seize the unwary traveller and carry him down into the peaty brown depths; the wee folk chattering behind a waterfall so that you could easily hear their voices, laughing like girls, but you never saw them, or if you did, things would go ill with you. Dyer, for all his hard-bitten Australian exterior, was superstitious. He had felt strange sensations in lonely places in the outback, and later discovered they were Aborigine burial grounds or corroboree sites.

His mother had been Highland, which was why he had come here, and perhaps that was why he felt slightly uneasy now that he was alone with the powers of this ancient land;

the Sgurr behind him – it really did seem to be almost leaning over him, the Ballagan Burn to his right chattering harmlessly among the rocks and mini-waterfalls. Burns and rivers were supposed to have spirits of their own and some of them demanded human sacrifices. He remembered a rhyme his mother had read to him years ago out of a long lost story book:

"Bloodthirsty Dee
Each year needs three."

It was late now and there was a chill in the air – an un-Australian chill. The sun had set in cotton wool behind the three blue peaks and the sky to the west was turning from red to dark purple-grey.

"The clouds have spirits too," he had heard his mother say.

It was exactly a month later that Fraser found the dying otter.

KWARUTTA'S CURSE

For a week Fraser flushed his medicine, day by day, down the toilet. For a week he waited uneasily for the tumblings of the mind to return. For a week he heard only chirrups and squeaks and barks from his former friends.

Then one night, at dead of night, he woke. It was hot and still and a shaft of moonlight slanted across his bed. He sat up. What had wakened him? He went to the window and opened it.

Then he heard it. "A kill! A mole." It was Nephesh the owl calling to his mate.

Fraser tried his own voice, "Nephesh!" and to his delight the word came out in the dialect of the birds of prey. "Nephesh, what moves?"

"Nothing moves," Nephesh replied automatically through half closed beak as he carried the mole back to his mate on the nest. Then, as an afterthought, "Who asks?"

"The boy with the bird's tongue." Fraser had never got round to giving himself a name in the language of the animals.

"Ooh! We thought you had gone away. The geese said you must have migrated. Do you migrate?"

"I suppose so." Fraser hadn't thought about it like that before. "Yes, of course I do. But I'm back now. Tell One-eye. Tell Barook."

Fraser realised that Nephesh would know nothing about the illnesses which might affect an otter, but the two animals might and he wanted to ask them.

Nephesh wheeled away into the night calling, "I will tell them."

Fraser thought that he would never get back to sleep in his excitement, but the next thing he knew it was bright hard morning and a pair of jackdaws were quarrelling over some bacon rind they had found somewhere.

"Leave it; it's mine."

"No! Mine! Mine! Mine!"

This sort of argument was common enough, but Fraser listened in delight for he hadn't heard anything like it for a year and he felt like a traveller come home after a long exile in a country where he couldn't speak the language.

"Hey boys!" he called. "What moves?"

The two stopped, startled.

Then one began again, as if expecting that Fraser would settle the argument. "I found it first. He's a thief, thief, thief!"

Fraser left them to it, simply rejoicing in having rediscovered his secret language. He spent the rest of that day discussing worms with a group of starlings and the garden blackbird, passing the time of day with a pair of yellowhammers and trying to persuade a rabbit that he was really harmless and only wanted to talk to him.

"Can't be too careful," quivered the rabbit. "Stoats and weasels can turn on the charm too, you know; talk as if they were offering you buttercups, and then, when you're off your guard..." He shook all over at the thought of what had happened to a kinsman of his who had not been on his guard.

That evening, in the gloaming, Fraser stole into the woods following the path by which One-eye had led him on the morning he had released Barook from the trap.

As he wound along the trail far into the deep woods he tried the call. "One-eye, Barook, what moves? It is the boy with the beast's tongue who asks."

For a long time there was no answer and Fraser was almost ready to give up when, from some dense cover in the shadows, came the reply:

"Boy with our tongue, it is One-eye who answers." The old fox slunk forward and stared at the boy with his one eye. "So you've come back. The birds said you had migrated, but I know that men do not migrate. I thought you were dead. Barook howled the death howl for you."

"How is Barook?" asked Fraser.

"Poor Barook," snorted One-eye. "He's well enough, eating worms and slugs. Thinks he's got a tit-bit if he catches a frog. He'll be glad to hear you're still alive. He hoped you were only hibernating, but he thought that by now you must be dead."

"One-eye," confided Fraser now that his relationship with the animal and the old familiarity had been re-established, "a week ago an otter died. He was poisoned. I couldn't speak his language. Do you know what happened to him?"

"So the otter died," repeated One-eye thoughtfully. "He came up from the pools below the woods. Decided to change his hunting grounds and fish Kwarutta's pool. I told him that would be bad luck. Kwarutta killed all that was in it and then was killed himself. Now the fish are dying and the frogs and toads and newts are leaving. The water birds are going too, those that came back after Kwarutta was killed. Nothing lives there any more."

"Why are they dying?" Fraser whispered.

"The water smells bad," said the fox. "I wouldn't drink it or eat anything that came out of it. Some of the birds say it's Kwarutta's curse. Or perhaps it's some new trick of your people to kill off the wood folk."

Fraser had no answer to that.

THE HAUNTING

Dyer crouched in his caravan. The yellow calor gas light let him read and write. There were noises in the night all around; the howl of the wind; the rushing and gurgling of the burn outside.

The wind came and went, like a sick man gasping for breath. In the strongest gusts the caravan shook and Dyer decided that he would have to anchor it more securely in the morning. Then he heard another sound, above the wind and the chattering of the burn; an unearthly yell like nothing he had ever heard before.

For a moment his mother's Highland blood spoke to him of kelpies, but his brash Australian common sense soon reasserted itself and he turned over and went to sleep.

The next morning was clear, the sky washed clean of cloud and the three blue peaks looking so close Dyer felt that he could reach out and touch them. This was a scene he had to paint, and to get the foreground he wanted he decided to take his easel down the Range Rover Track for several hundred yards, out of sight of the caravan, till the reflection of the peaks was mirrored exactly on the still surface of the loch and the houses of Dunadd crouched like brightly painted toys.

He was there all day. When he returned in the early evening he saw at once that something was wrong.

The caravan had moved.

The wheels were no longer in line with the chockstones he had so carefully placed to keep them in position, and there were scratches in the paintwork he was sure had not been there in the morning. All around were the prints of cloven hooves as if a flock of sheep or a herd of deer – or devils – had danced around the caravan.

And so a pattern was set; by night that unearthly howling; by day, whenever Dyer left the van, scratches and signs that it had been moved slightly; sometimes at night grey ghosts of mist would rise from nowhere and crawl and swirl over the moor so that everything was veiled and muffled and a rock would suddenly loom as if it were alive, like a… kelpie?

But there wasn't a lot of mist about that summer. The June heatwave lasted through July and local people told Dyer that he didn't realise how lucky he had been. The burn grumbled quietly to itself among its rocks and pools and Dyer couldn't imagine the slope above his site turning into the waterfall that Archie had predicted and sweeping his van away.

"Locals are always like that," he thought. "Like to exaggerate the dangers of where they live, just to impress tourists."

In fact Dyer now found himself with the opposite problem – how to collect enough water. But this was something he knew about from his expeditions in the Nullarbor Plain in South Australia, and he soon had sunk jerry cans in the burn and the bogs in places where they would collect all he needed.

KWARUTTA'S POOL

The dry weather did not suit everyone.

Hobdax the hedgehog had a lean time of it because slugs and other soft creatures that need to stay moist, burrowed deep and kept well out of the way so that he had difficulty in finding them; Barook had to use his claws and dig deeper than he could ever remember.

Klamath the heron fared better. He patrolled the wetlands below Sebek's pool and, although frogs were hard to find, there were always enough fish to keep him going. Sebek himself ignored the hot weather; his pool would never dry out.

Those who liked to hunt dry footed were in their element. One-eye prowled the trails of the wood, nose to the ground, for scents lie long when there is no rain to wash them away. Cruach the cat was out on the moor every night. Happiest of all was Eye of the Wind soaring endlessly and effortlessly in the rising currents of hot air.

In the middle of the month the real drought set in. The wind settled in the east and brought a brown haze down on the land. The sky burned blue-hot day after day. The smaller burns shrivelled to the tiniest of trickles and even the fat peat bogs on the moor began to dry out, leaving cracked and caked crusts where there was usually soft mud.

Only the Ballagan Burn still carried a little water and only the two biggest pools, Sebek's and Kwarutta's, remained deep enough for the bigger fish. There they bellied down into the mud and showed scarcely enough energy to rise for the water boatmen skating over the surface or the midges dancing in clouds just above it.

It was during this time that Fraser set out to discover what had poisoned the otter. From what One-eye had told him he realised that whatever it was had come from Kwarutta's pool. This was the highest pool in the wood. Beyond it the Ballagan Burn crawled through a gap in the boundary wall which separated the wood from the moor. Kwarutta had killed or driven away everything that had lived in or around the pool, but after he had died they had quickly re-colonised the place, for there were plenty of insects and plants and the feeding was good.

Here Fraser came on his mission. Water creatures were, he knew, difficult to talk to. A shiver still ran down his spine when he remembered his meeting with Sebek the pike in the lower pool.

"Perhaps," he thought, "the best thing would be to settle down and listen and try to understand whatever I hear.

So he squatted down on a big square stone which had fallen from the ruined cottage that stood beside the water, tried to shut out the silly chattering of the birds, and listened for the noises from the depths of the pool.

There was a whirring of insect wings as big blue dragonflies hunted like hawks across the surface and wild bees droned round flowers in the patches of sunlight between the trees.

There were plops and splashes as stickleback and perch came up and gulped for air and the rustle of reeds as larger fish nosed among their roots. All this was unintelligible to Fraser, so he settled down sleepily to wait for something more.

Then he saw the stain. Like a big snake lying in wait, it meandered lazily, green and brown, from the inlet burn across the far end of the pool.

There was also the smell. The pool was already beginning to dry out and the caking mud at the edges gave off a sharp-sour smell. Perhaps that was what One-eye, whose nose was a hundred times keener than any human's, had meant when he said that the water smelled bad.

It was hot and still and stuffy and smelly. The droning and the buzzing drummed a dreamy sort of sleep upon Fraser and he began to feel again that tumbling of the mind…

When he wakened he was lying by the side of the pool, almost at eye level with the water. He could see the water boatmen on the surface and below them a diving beetle with its bright silver bubble of air under its tail and tiny leeches twisting like wires on the bottom.

With one ear to the ground he could hear the shaking of moles in their tunnels and with the other the lapping of the water and the soft voices of the creatures in it. He lay still, trying to breathe short and shallow so as not to disturb their talk.

"What's the matter with the water? I can't breathe." An elderly trout flipped his tail weakly and gulped air in desperation.

A newt under a stone on the bank turned a goggle eye in the direction of the fish. "I don't know. I've had to come out."

The newt could, of course, live on land but he always felt uncomfortable there and it was reluctantly that he had crawled out of the pool, his skin burning and his eyes nipping.

"All right for you," gasped the trout, "but I'm stuck here."

"Not really," said the newt. "The water seems to be better downstream, as far as I can see. I'm going to try it once I've got my breath back. Why don't you get out of here and take your chance in the burn?"

"Looks too shallow, with the water as low as this."

57

"Well, its worth a try. Anything's better than suffocating here. Give your tail a flip and get moving."

Fraser understood most of this, although the dialect was strange to someone used to the talk of birds and small animals and the voices were very soft. He wondered if they would be able to understand him, or would speak to him, since most of their enemies came from the world outside the water.

"What moves?" he called, trying to imitate the accent of the fish.

"This moves," grunted the trout, obviously unaware of who had actually spoken to him. "This scum moves, and it stinks, and it suffocates. Who asks?"

"Just someone on the bank," replied Fraser, hoping the fish could not see how big he was.

However, the trout was not alarmed. He probably thought that Fraser was some kind of wading bird for he went on, "Can't you see for yourself? This dark stain is taking away our breath. Those who have legs or wings have gone long ago. Some of the smaller fish, minnows and sticklebacks have taken their chance in the shallows and got out of the pool, but I'm a fair size and I can't do that easily."

Gasping with the exertion of this speech, the big fish settled belly deep in the mud like an elderly invalid taking to bed for good.

Gently Fraser reached down and touched him. "Do what the newt said. There's better water down stream. Go for it. Don't let yourself be trapped in this poisonous place."

In desperation the trout summoned the energy to lash with his tail until he surged through the weeds and over the bar at the bottom end of the pool. Here the water was just deep enough for him, and he half swam, half wriggled until he reached a stretch where he could settle comfortably below the surface. Here the water seemed to be fresher for almost at once the fish livened up and Fraser saw him rise to take an insect from the surface.

Until now Fraser had not dared to move. Now he stood up unsteadily, his head throbbing so that he had to hold on to the branch of a willow that overhung the pool. He knew what he must do. As One-eye had said, the water was poisoned. The fish and the frogs couldn't be expected to know where the poison had come from, but one creature surely would. The only one who knew about all the burns and pools in the district was Klamath the heron. Fraser had to find him.

KLAMATH THE HERON

Klamath the heron was too big to do much flying. He had long legs to wade through shallow water and a long neck with a beak a foot long to snatch fish or frogs with a single dart. What he was best at was standing motionless with a patience One-eye or Cruach could never have matched, until something moved in his line of strike, and then the big beak did the rest.

He could fly when he needed to, of course, and he had to in order to reach his nest, a big untidy affair at the top of a tree at the very bottom of the wood, near Sebek's pool, handy for the wetlands and the shore of the loch.

His other reason for flying was to change his fishing grounds and when he felt like doing this he would take off with a jump, coil his long neck back and fly with powerful sweeps of his big grey wings at a very fair speed.

When the water was low he would often do this. He didn't go far. He was no goose to set off on marathons to the other side of the world. Klamath knew where all the pools and burns were between the shore of the loch and the Sgurr and he flew on precise expeditions to definite destinations.

Only he didn't fish within the woods – his wings were too broad to manoeuvre among the branches; so the two biggest pools, Sebek's and Kwarutta's, were places he never visited.

As that stifling July scorched on and the burn dropped and the pools dried out, the toads hid under stones and the frogs buried themselves in the mud. As Klamath strode the shrunken water even the fish lay low and were difficult to find.

Then, once every day or two, he would dive into the air and flap his way over the wood and up above the moor to visit some lonely lochan or the upper reaches of the burn to decide where it might be worth coming down to try his luck. But the fishing was never good enough for it to be worth his while to come back. It was just after one of these expeditions when he had returned to patrol the shore of the loch that he met Fraser.

"What moves?" asked the boy.

"Not much. The water's too low. Besides, it's tainted. There's something in it."

"I hear the fish are dying upstream."

"The water's all right up on the moor," answered Klamath. "No decent fish up there though. It's not too bad down here; just a taint."

"The fish are dying in the pools in the woods."

"I don't go there. But there *is* something new on the moor above the woods; a man's house, and yet not really a house; it's on wheels, like a tractor. Anyway he's putting something in the burn. That's what's killing the fish. I went close for a look, but the smell was foul. I wouldn't eat anything that came out of that stretch of the burn."

"A house on wheels," thought Fraser. "A caravan, perhaps. On the moor? I wonder where."

RONA

Rona, the vet nurse, was walking Sandy, her big yellow labrador, when he met her. Once or twice, since he had brought the otter to her, Fraser had wondered whether to tell her that animals can talk and that he could talk to them. She wasn't like Jim Douglas, she loved animals, but then she was a lot older than he was and might not take him seriously.

When he did let her into his secret, it was by accident.

Sandy, running ahead of his mistress, came bounding towards Fraser, all paws and tail. The boy had serious matters on his mind just then and without thinking, instead of the usual "Good boy," gave him "What moves?" in the accent he would have used towards One-eye.

The effect was spectacular. The dog braked to a halt, all four paws spread out, cocked his ears and put his head on one side in a puzzled way.

"Was that you?" he asked.

Fraser didn't feel he could deny it. "Yes. What moves?"

"Where did you learn that trick?" Unlike the wild animals, Sandy knew enough about human beings to be quite certain that, lovable as they were as playmates, unfortunately they could not talk. "Not even my mistress can do that."

"Some birds taught me when I was in hospital."

"Birds!" Sandy seemed disappointed. "They're not worth talking to."

Then an idea struck him and he became so excited that he chased his tail three times round before sitting down in front of Fraser expectantly. "Could you teach my mistress?

She's quite intelligent and I think she understands a lot of what I say to her."

By this time Rona had caught up, clearly baffled. At first it had seemed to her that Fraser and Sandy were barking and growling at each other and she wondered if the boy was teasing the dog. But as she got closer she could see, from his excited jumping and the flailing of his tail that Sandy was delighted about something.

"Hi there," she called to Fraser and then, as the excited dog continued to bark and jump about, "Sandy, quiet now. Calm down."

"It's OK," said Fraser. "He's talking to me."

"I know, but he's not supposed to bark like that."

"Then he couldn't talk to me."

"Of course he could. Dogs talk with their tail and their ears. It's called body language."

By this time Sandy was completely out of control, bounding round in circles, jumping up on the boy and the girl and making a noise that sounded to Rona like a mixture of a growl, a whine and a yelp. Fraser felt that he needed to prove himself. Anyway it would be OK to tell Rona. She would take him seriously now.

"Will I tell you what he's saying?"

First he calmed the dog. "Your mistress doesn't believe we can talk to each other. So sit still for a minute and I'll explain."

Sandy lay down with his big brown nose between his paws. Fraser switched to human words. "He says he didn't know humans could learn to talk. He says he thinks you're quite clever and could I teach *you* to talk?"

The girl laughed. "What an imagination you've got!"

"You think I'm kidding?"

He turned to the dog and they exchanged a series of yelps, barks and whines. Fraser translated: "He says you walked him across a field with cows in it this morning. He

63

says that a fox had passed that way just before sunrise; he picked up the scent quite clearly. He says," more barks and yelps from Sandy, "that you let him off the lead and he got into a burn and got muddy. Then he chased a rabbit – nearly caught it, he says. Is that true?"

Rona's eyes were wide with amazement. "How did you know that? You must have seen us."

"No. He just told me. Do you want me to ask him anything?"

"Ask him who stole the cold ham mum left on the table last night."

Fraser obliged with a few growls and grunts.

The answer was unmistakable, even to a human who couldn't understand the language. The dog stood up with his ears flat against his head and his tail curved between his legs, whined a few abject apologies and pushed a big wet nose into Rona's hand for forgiveness.

"He says it was him. He's very sorry," translated Fraser unnecessarily.

Rona was almost convinced. "Tell him I'm not angry anymore."

Fraser obliged again and the forgiven thief jumped up with a joyful bark and began licking his mistress' face.

Then it was time for serious human talk.

While Sandy roamed on ahead and periodically reported back to Fraser on what animals had been there before them from the scents they had left behind, Rona was full of questions. How much could Fraser understand? What could he say to the animals? What animals had he spoken to? What did they tell him? How had he learned to speak their language?

The last question worried him. Fraser didn't know how he had come by his gift. But he did know that he had first had it after driving down that road in France with the sunlight flashing through the poplars – the flashing light, the tumbling of his mind. And he knew that he had lost it when he had taken the pills the consultant had given him.

He also knew how he had got it back again. But this he did not tell her.

"But Fraser, you're cured. You're all right now. So how have you got the speech back?"

"I don't know."

"But if you're only able to speak to the animals when you're sick, you must be sick now!"

"I stopped taking the pills," Fraser admitted grudgingly.

"You mustn't; you've got to go on taking them always; you could be seriously ill. Does your mum know?"

Fraser was determined. "You musn't tell mum. I've got to find out what killed the otter."

"Does that really matter?"

"The fish are dying; the frogs have had to leave the water. You're a vet; don't you care?"

Rona did care; more than that she was fascinated by Fraser's wonderful talent and realised how valuable it would be to a vet; but Fraser might be risking his health, perhaps even his life and she knew that he would have to give up his gift.

She also knew that he understood the animals in a way that neither she nor Cathy could ever really appreciate; so she struck a bargain with him.

She would help him to find the "house on wheels", as Klamath had put it, and whatever poison was coming from it. And when they found out she would tell Cathy who would know what to do about it.

Until then Fraser would use his ability to converse with the animals to get as much information as possible. But once the mystery was solved and the poison cleared away he would start taking his medicine again and would promise her that he would never, ever stop taking it.

FLIGHT FOR LIFE

This meant another expedition for Fraser.

There was no point in going back to Kwarutta's pool. According to Klamath the trouble in the burn started further up, on the moor above the wood. So that was where to start; at the point where the burn tumbled through a hole in the wall that divided the wood from the moor, near the spot where he had first seen Eye of the Wind.

To get to the edge of the wood he had to follow a trail that ran beside the upper reaches of the burn and this was worse than what he had seen already. Stains in strange colours sagged gently downstream and here and there were the silver bellies of upturned, dead fish.

Then he was over the wall and on to the open moor. He had been up there once before, the day he had clambered up to the foot of the crags of Sgurr Mor and had met the eagle face to face.

It was very hot and still and a dull haze hung over the moor so that, although the sky was clear, Fraser could scarcely make out the ghostly outline of the Sgurr.

The place stank. The burn dropped across the moor in a series of steps with little waterfalls and deep rock pools succeeding each other. In the pools there was the same coloured scum and Fraser couldn't see any water boatmen on the surface. The waterfalls had dried up to a drip and the rocks on either side were plastered with a dry, grey, papery substance that seemed to have dried onto them.

Fraser climbed up the bank, taking care not to touch the grey stuff – just in case. After about ten minutes he heard a noise above him and was able to see, on the other side of the burn, perched dizzily above him, a small caravan, and, leading to it, like a fresh wound in the side of the hill, the new Range Rover Track.

As he watched, a man came out of the caravan with a basin in his hands and walked over to the edge of the burn, just above a point where it plummeted fifteen feet clear into a rock pool. The hands came up, the basin tilted and the water launched itself like a diving snake into space to splash against the rocks below.

Dyer turned and disappeared back into the van.

Fraser climbed closer for a better look. Surely a basin-full of dirty dishwater wouldn't kill fish?

Then the man re-appeared, carrying something heavy with difficulty. He balanced it on the ledge above the fifteen foot drop. This, whatever it was, Fraser realised must be the cause of the poisoning further downstream.

"Stop!" he screamed.

Dyer looked up in surprise.

"Don't! You're poisoning the fish."

Dyer ignored him and tipped the contents of the container over the edge.

Fraser was wild with anger. "Murderer!" he yelled. "You killed the otter and the fish and the frogs."

"Sod off, Sonny," growled Dyer.

"You're killing animals. You're a murderer." Fraser danced with rage.

"I said sod off," Dyer snarled, "before I put my toe on your backside," and he took a step forward.

"Murderer! Rotten rat!" Fraser turned and fled as the Australian jumped the burn and bounded towards him across the hillside.

He fled for his life down that steep slope; rocks and heather and black peat leaped at him from left and right;

rowan branches slapped his face; and then the bracken; he was floundering head high in the bracken like in one of those nightmares when you have to run for your life and find yourself rooted to the spot.

The speed, the dizziness, the helplessness were all so much like the tumblings of his mind that Fraser was afraid he would black out, to be pounced on, not this time by rooks, but by that murderous ogre who, he knew, was only a strangler's step behind him.

He didn't black out, but just as he was almost in reach of the boundary wall of the wood he landed awkwardly on a loose stone, felt his ankle turn sickeningly and fell, face down, with his mouth full of ferns.

THE GOAT TRAIL

Bhuiridh*, the bearded, shaggy-coated patriarch, surveyed his domain and his subjects. From a rock overlooking the sparse scrubland of the lower moor he watched for any sign of a challenge to his authority, and his magnificent scimitar horns signalled a threat to anyone foolhardy enough to dispute his rights. That one horn had been broken off near the tip was proof that they were not for ornament.

His six wives grazed docilely under the protection of those horns and the jealous stare of his yellow eyes. His innumerable children, grandchildren and great-grandchildren rooted and pawed and bleated in the coarse hill grass.

The other billy goats knew their places, and he tolerated them; even Gobhar# who had once almost dared to challenge his position and would probably one day succeed him; but that day was a long way off. No hunter, fox, wild cat or even eagle, dared approach the flock openly and tradition on the moor related that Bhuiridh had once driven a fully antlered stag off his territory.

Several times a month, as the mood moved him, Bhuiridh led his six wives and the camp followers of his flock along the ancient goat trail that led from the woods across the Ballagan Burn and up on to the higher parts of the moor.

Bhuiridh's predecessor, whom he had defeated and deposed in a bitter skull-butting battle so long ago that no-

* pronounced Vooree
# pronounced Gower

one else remembered, had done the same. And so had that predecessor's predecessor.

Sometimes, in severe winter weather, deer, coming down from the top of the moor, used the trail, but normally they kept to higher ground; and in the traditions of the animals of the moor it was known simply as 'the Goat Trail'.

Man respected it too. It was too steep and rough for the ponies that used to bring down the carcasses of stags shot on the hill and they used a gentler route. The tracks crossed at one point, just beyond the Ballagan Burn, but men and goats march to different rhythms and they seldom met.

Recently, Bhuiridh had noted, the pony track had been widened for a new beast of burden that growled and whined ferociously as it took the steep gradient. But that traffic, too, was occasional and posed no threat to his authority.

Sometimes, in his long experience as leader of the flock, Bhuiridh had known the track to become blocked; a fall of rock after a severe storm had washed away the footholds of the boulders, had covered it for a while. But the goats had picked their way through the obstacles and eventually the biggest boulders had worked loose again and trundled further down the slope till they lodged against the boundary wall of the wood.

Very long ago, so tradition on the moor told, a new man, an incomer who did not know the customs of the country, had built a fence across the track. But the goats had leaned and shoved and scratched and levered and in time the fence posts had come out and the wires had snapped, the fence had fallen and the goats had resumed their immemorial pathway.

So now the presence of a man-made thing, a small cottage on wheels, didn't concern Bhuiridh. At present it was possible to go round it; eventually it would rot away and break up; or the autumn floods would wash it away; or the winter winds would hurl it across the hillside.

The younger billies felt differently; too young to see things in the long term as Bhuiridh could, they saw the caravan as a challenge; it had no right to be there; it must be moved; and hard skulls and horns were the tools for this kind of work.

Gobhar, in particular, saw this as his opportunity to gain in status and prestige. If old Bhuiridh couldn't lead the flock any more when there was an enemy to be faced, then perhaps it was time for a change in leadership and he, Gobhar, would not be afraid to take up the challenge in the time-honoured custom of the goats – head on.

Bhuiridh was well aware of this challenge to his leadership. He knew that the things men make are for the moment, lasting only until they go chasing off after a new idea. But a challenge to his leadership was another matter. His horns were the mightiest; his strength was the greatest; he would lead by example.

RETREAT

Fraser waited, doomed, for the grasp of heavy hands at his throat. Or perhaps the end would come with a knife or an axe or a gun.

But nothing happened.

His ankle was sore. He couldn't run; probably he couldn't even walk. Fearfully he turned his head and looked behind him. The moor was blank. The ogre was gone. The immediate danger was over, but Fraser still faced a painful hobble home with one ankle feeling as if it was packed with little sharp needles which stabbed a hundred ways whenever he put any weight on it.

Slowly he went on, sometimes crawling on hands and knees, sometimes hopping on his one good foot, over the wall and away from the moor; till he saw Kwarutta's pool, glinting like copper where the light chequered through the leaves and wondered if his tumblings of the mind would come back with the heat and the stench.

Then agonising along the trail through the wood, often having to rest from the pain, yet each time he stopped fancying he could hear, above his thumping heart, the faintest rustle, the slightest breathing as Something stalked him through the shadows of the trees in the gathering dusk.

When he held his breath to hear better, the Thing stopped breathing too. When he was forced to breathe again with deep gasps, he was sure that he heard its hot pant just behind that tree or the bush over there. And once he was so sure that he heard It gathering Itself for the final spring that would bring It on top of him that he leaped, one legged, in his terror into a bramble bush and fell, scarred and scraped, with the red scrawls of the thorns stinging on his skin.

But the blow never came; and at last he could see the lights in the windows of his home and he knew that, if it came to the worst, he was within shouting distance.

In fact Dyer, having made a demonstration of ferocity which had had the intended effect, had turned back with a chuckle, picked up the empty latrine of his chemical toilet, replaced it and sat back with a pipe and a dram to watch the sunset. Of course, by the conditions of his rental of the site, he should have buried the latrine's contents higher up on the moor, but that would have meant carrying the thing a hundred yards along the goat trail. In any case, you couldn't reasonably be expected to dig a hole in the baked clay of the dried out peat bogs. Dyer had only tried it once.

THE GREAT GALE

The heat and drought lasted another three days. Then with August came the thunder; at first distant rumblings as towering clouds massed over the hills; then the steady 'spit, spit' of big drops of rain; then the wind rose and the rain turned to hail as the full blast of the storm hit the van. It rocked and rattled under the bombardment, and the thunder cracked and the lightning flickered all around. But it stayed in place, held by the extra anchors Dyer had put in.

Then the mist closed in. It was as if the god of the storm realised that the fortress could not be taken by assault and that siege tactics would have to be employed. The thunder and lightning grew fainter and dimmer and faded away, the wind died down and the hail turned to rain, a steady drenching downpour.

By early evening the pools on the top of the moor were brimming and soon the whole hillside was awash as the water ran straight off the rock hard ground. Dyer had started to prepare his evening meal when he noticed the first trickle of water coming over the rocks above. At first he continued with his cooking, but the trickle became a torrent and the torrent a cascade and soon the whole ledge on which the van rested was awash and he could feel his home shudder under the force of the flood.

When he went outside to investigate he saw to his horror that part of the ledge and whole sections of the Range Rover Track were starting to collapse and crumble into a thick red paste, which was oozing onto the hillside below.

Then the van shifted and lurched as the ground to which it was anchored began to dissolve. Dyer decided to leave. A four mile hike in this downpour along the track while it was still light was something he could handle. But if the van turned over in the night, during the dark, with the track by then perhaps washed away... so he put on his boots, waterproof trousers and cagoule and slurped off down the crumbling pathway.

Tomorrow JCBs would be brought up to rebuild the track and the next day Archie would come up with the Range Rover and a squad of men to repair the damage to the caravan site.

* * *

Bhuiridh and his six wives and innumerable offspring huddled under trees and behind bushes in the lee of the boundary wall of the wood and rode out the storm. The Ballagan Burn threw itself like a rabid animal at the wall and by morning there was a gap six feet wide where there had been only a small opening the evening before. The level of Kwarutta's pool rose until it burst its banks and surges of angry water slapped against the stonework of the ruined cottage. The scums and stains were churned and scattered and spread far and wide as the whole wood became one wide river.

Further downstream burrows were flooded and mice and voles had to take their chance above ground and fly for their lives, while slower moving creatures like slow worms were drowned.

At the bottom of the wood Sebek's pool filled fuller than even he could ever remember until it too overflowed its boundaries and the force of the water falling from above churned up the peaty bottom until the water looked like cocoa.

And lowest of all, the wetlands beside the Loch flooded and Klamath stepped delicately to a delicious feast of frogs and fish flushed out from the mud and stones where they had been hiding.

THE CHALLENGE

The next day the cloud lifted a little and the downpour eased to a drizzle. Bhuiridh mustered his wives and his kinsmen and led them, as he had done for years, up the Goat Trail to their moorland pasture. When they reached the caravan they found it tilted precariously, one wheel overhanging what was left of the ledge. It was still blocking their ancient right of way. Bhuiridh stepped aside when he reached it; there was room enough to pass.

"I'd knock it over." The speaker was Gobhar. "It's got no right there. I wouldn't stand for it."

"It'll rot away in time," said Bhuiridh as he scavenged for anything edible that the flood water might have left.

"Scared to take it on then?" insinuated Gobhar. "Want me to do it for you?"

Three of Bhuiridh's wives and several younger females were watching with interest. Gobhar was a good-looking buck with fine, circling horns and a heavy mane and beard.

"Want me to show you how?" he repeated.

Four or five of the younger billies had gathered round by now, their interest in grazing temporarily suspended as the tension between champion and challenger riveted their attention.

"You can't teach me anything," Bhuiridh was scornful.

"Then get on with it or I'll do the job myself."

For a moment the two faced each other, foreheads lowered, horns swinging, like two boxers sparring for an opening. But Gobhar knew he wasn't ready to take on the older billy and Bhuiridh knew that he couldn't afford to lose face by standing back and letting his challenger topple the van.

"Here we go." He reared on his hind legs and then, with lowered head, crashed against the side of the van. His horns scratched the paintwork. Another heave and the van juddered and balanced, rocking like a logan stone. At this Gobhar rushed forward, charging the van and with a sudden creak of resignation it lurched over the edge of the platform and somersalted in leap after leap two hundred feet down the slope, until it lodged – what was left of it – against the strong trunk of a mountain ash.

Dyer, toiling up from Kilrasken on foot to inspect the night's damage, was appalled to see the savage horned heads of the two goats staring down as his home toppled and careered to destruction.

Had he come back after dark he would have heard the eerie cry as Cruach hunted over the very spot where he had slept for two months.

THE PROMISE

Fraser's ankle had only been sprained and, at the time, that had seemed a small price to pay for not having been chopped up and eaten alive by the murderous ogre of the moor. As soon as he could escape from his mum's worried fussing and could walk without too much pain he went to see Rona.

"I've found out who's poisoning the water," he told her and went on to explain about Dyer's caravan and the new road on the moor.

Rona told Cathy and Cathy, after checking that such a road and caravan did exist, phoned the Department of Environmental Health at the offices of the District Council. The Department sent two men in a van as far as they could go, but, as they told Cathy later, the road had been washed away, bits of the van were smashed and scattered over the moor like a plane wreck and a flock of wild goats was browsing contentedly where Dyer had hoped to make his home. They had also taken samples of water from the Ballagan Burn and it was now free from pollution. Dyer himself went away, possibly believing that there were, after all, spirits in the Burn and the Sgurr and the clouds.

All this information Rona passed on to Fraser, but when he started to go into a triumphal victory chant – "Serves him right! He'd no right to…" she cut him short.

"Fraser, there's something you must promise me."

"Oh, Oh!"

"You've solved the mystery?"

"Uhuh."

"Then you must promise me that you'll start taking your medicine again."

"All right."

"And you musn't ever again stop taking it."

"Ever?"

"Not ever!"

"I suppose so. Rona?"

"What is it?"

"Where's Sandy?"

The big labrador bounded up and the girl who loved animals listened in envy and sadness as Fraser had his last conversation with a four-footed creature.

THE MADNESS
OF THE WOLVES

THE DEAD TIME

After it was all over Fraser realised that it had started with the strange white ship; a tall ship with three masts like pine trees and a tangle of ropes and spars and sails. It had anchored in the loch late one evening and in the morning had been gone; like a ghost ship, Fraser had thought.

Jim Douglas, who had been out fishing with his dad that night, said the men on board "talked funny", but then Jim thought that folk from Glasgow talked funny.

Fraser did not see the ship; from his bedroom window the view to that part of the loch was blocked by the tall trees of the wood and now that his illness had come back so seriously, he was not allowed to leave the house – ever. Klamath the heron brought him the news of what was happening in the animal world around him, and it was Klamath who told him that an animal of some kind – Klamath thought it might have been a small dog – had been thrown overboard.

It was October, the coldest and driest anyone could remember. There was little wind and most of the leaves hung on the trees instead of falling to the ground to rot, and they burned gold and yellow and chestnut brown like the rich cloaks of kings in a book Fraser had been looking at. A few days later the first flotilla of wild geese arrived on the wetlands below the wood, exhausted after their long flight from their summer grounds in Iceland.

The geese were an unusual lot. They actually *wanted* to spend the winter at Dunadd.

Most birds and animals definitely did not. They called winter the Dead Time and those who could, avoided having to live through it. The swifts and swallows had gone long ago, following the summer south into Africa where there would be plenty of delicious insects to take on the wing.

Those who could not fly away got ready for the Dead Time in other ways. Hobdax the hedgehog had been preparing for weeks. He had put on a lot of weight and now dug deep into a bank of fallen leaves, rolled himself into a ball and settled down comfortably to sleep the winter away. The squirrels did the same; they had eaten as much as they could when food was plentiful early in the autumn and had hidden as much again away in secret stores; now they settled down in trees to drowse through the worst of the hard times ahead.

The hares and the stoats and, up on the high moors, the ptarmigan turned white as if expecting that the whole of the Dead Time would be spent wrapped in a blanket of snow.

THE WOLVES' PROMISE

It was one of the stoats who first realised that there was something far wrong in the wood.

"The weasels have gone mad," he told One-eye as they followed different scents one bitterly cold night.

At first the old fox thought nothing of the matter for it is well known in the woods that stoats and weasels dislike each other. Perhaps it has something to do with the weasels' envy of the stoats' winter coat; and of course those who wear a white fur which stands out, as an old weasel joke puts it "like a seagull in a rookery", do not like to be laughed at.

But after a while One-eye began to notice for himself; firstly there were the bodies of dead weasels lying along the trails with jaws agape and glazed eyes open; then there were the shrill sounds of bitter fighting among the living weasels; and occasionally One-eye would see one of them running in circles furiously, squealing in rage and fear.

Then the fox, oldest of all the hunters of the wood, remembered something his father had told him, something which had been passed down by *his* father in turn; something from so long ago that no living fox or badger or wild cat had ever met it and not even Eye of the Wind, the eagle who lives forever, knew of a case in his lifetime.

"It's the Madness of the Wolves," One-eye confided to Fraser. The boy and the fox had struck up a friendship since Fraser's illness had returned and he had had to come back to the cottage, an invalid unable to leave his room.

Fraser regularly threw tit-bits saved from meal times out

of his window at night and One-eye, older and stiffer as each season passed, was glad to share with him, especially in the Dead Time, although, as a young fox, he would have been far too proud to scavenge for man's leftovers. Fraser, in turn, was glad of the company and the news of all that was happening in places he could no longer visit himself.

So now One-eye, gratefully snapping up some crusts and a chunk of corned beef, explained to Fraser: "It is an old story; older than any of us now living. At the beginning of things when the Father of Kelpies was preparing the lochs and the woods and the moors he put all the birds and the animals and the fish in their places and told them how to hunt or graze and find food for themselves and their young.

But one of the animals, the Father of Wolves, said, 'I will not hunt as you have told me. I will kill as I wish. I will kill man's tame animals. I will kill man himself if I can. I will do as I please.'

The Father of Kelpies was angry at this and he turned to the Father of Wolves, 'For what you have said I will curse you. Your people will become many and strong and will be able to kill man's beasts and even man himself. Men will be afraid of you as they will fear no other animal. But they will hunt you and trap you and poison you. And one day, at last they will tame the lightning and hunt you with it so that all your people will be destroyed.'

"'Very well,' snarled the Father of Wolves. 'Let man and wolf kill each other in fair fight. But if you let men tame the lightning that will not be fair. What will you give to my people to even the score?'

The Father of Kelpies thought for a moment, pawed the turf as if he was digging for an answer and then shook his yellow mane. 'To you I will give a weapon more terrible than the tame lightning. To you I will give a power to kill – for that is what you seem to want – beyond anything you can imagine. To you I will give the Madness.

'Once in a while one of your people will go mad and will run over the moors and through the woods biting everything that comes in his way. Then he will die, but everything he has bitten will go mad in its turn, dog and fox, wild cat and badger, and they will run, spreading death through the trails and tunnels and burrows of the woods, and, this I make as a special promise to you, in their madness they will not be afraid to bite man himself; and every man bitten, even to the slightest graze, will go mad himself and will die.

'I promise this power of death to your children.'

'Good,' said the Father of Wolves. 'The odds are fair. I accept the venom of the madness for my people against the tame lightning you give to my enemy.'"

One-eye stopped and snuffled around hungrily. Fraser threw out some more crusts and a hunk of cheese.

"And that is what happened." One-eye finished the food. "The weapon was given to the wolves. From time to time one of them would go mad and run amok – afraid of nothing – biting and killing by poison like Seti the adder, and man and his dogs suffered and so did we of the woods.

"But the Father of Kelpies remembered the other part of his promise and gave to the enemy – to your people – the tame lightning.

"How we have all suffered from that! And his curse on the wolves also came true. The last of the wolves has been killed and the last carriers of the madness died so long ago that we thought that the old war between wolves and men was over. We were glad, for the tame lightning that men carry is terrible, but the madness is worse. Now the curse brought upon us all by the Father of Wolves has come back. It is killing the weasels and every creature a weasel bites is infected and carries the curse. Warn your people." One-eye shook himself. That had been a long speech for an animal. "Warn your people," he repeated and bounded off.

JET

Jim Douglas took up the story. He came round to see Fraser after school one day, bubbling with excitement.

"Jet! You mind Jet, the black tomcat? Yesterday he went for dad. Jumped at him and bit his hand. Then, know what? Dad locked mum and me in the house and got the gun. Then he went and shot Jet. Then he went to see the doctor and he sent him to hospital. Lot of fuss over a scratch."

Jim didn't seem particularly upset about the death of one of the farm cats, but then there were lots of cats on the farm.

"Funny thing, though. They got Cathy the vet to come and take Jet's body away. I'd just have dug a hole for it."

Fraser realised that Jim had not been told the whole story.

"Oh, another thing. There was this weird dog. We heard this howling all night and in the morning here was this dog dead outside the front door. Cathy took it away too. Funny sort of dog."

"How?" asked Fraser.

"Sort of long-legged. Funny colour – yellowish. I never saw a dog like that before." Jim added a few stories about Misty and Tess killing rats in the barn and then went off home for his tea.

That night Fraser threw a lot of tit-bits out of his bedroom window in the hope that One-eye would turn up and give his version of these events, but his only visitor was Nephesh the owl.

"What moves, Nephesh?"

"Strange times," answered the owl. "The game are uneasy. The weasels have all gone mad and all the other folk in the burrows are disturbed. I don't remember a time like it since I learned to fly."

"Do you know anything about a strange yellow dog?" asked Fraser.

"There was one, a newcomer to our territory, howling all night not long ago. There must have been something wrong with it. I think it died."

Nephesh couldn't add anything to this and had never heard the story One-eye had told the other night.

"Madness of the wolves? What is a wolf? Your farm dogs are mad enough that run about all day in the sun. And so are the weasels just now, running about slavering and biting everything in sight. I've stopped eating them – though they're easy enough to catch, the way they are." Nephesh flapped off to hunt for something which still behaved normally.

RABIES!

The next week was frustrating for Fraser. Trapped behind the glass prison of his window with a view to the garden he could not walk in and the trees he could not climb, he had to wait until people or animals or birds came to him with news. And when the news they brought did not tell him what he wanted to know and he had to wait in the hope that another visitor would appear with the missing pieces of the jigsaw, he longed to be able to get up and wander at will along the wood trails until he found what he was looking for, or some bird or animal who could tell him.

One-eye came to visit regularly these cold, cruel nights, but the more he came to rely on the boy's leftovers, the less hunting he did and the less news he had to offer.

Nephesh was about most nights and by day there were all the birds of the garden – blackbirds, starlings, magpies, jackdaws – and Klamath flew overhead from time to time on his way to fresh fishing grounds, but apart from Nephesh none of them knew much about what was going on in the wood.

There were human visitors too, of course. His mum and dad were there every day, but their talk of the business of adults in Dunadd or Glasgow didn't interest Fraser. Jim Douglas came occasionally when he had some particularly exciting information to share, but Jim was bored by being indoors – he said he had enough of it at school – and never stayed very long.

So it was to Rona, the vet nurse, that Fraser had to turn for more news of the strange goings on in the wood and around the farms. She visited him regularly, usually bringing Sandy, and then Fraser found himself translating between dog and girl while Rona could only look on in envy of his gift of talking with animals.

One day she came alone. "Do you know what rabies is?" she asked him.

Fraser had never heard the word.

"It's a horrible disease. Animals get it and they run about biting other animals and that spreads it. Sometimes animals with rabies bite people and if the people get the disease from them they usually die."

"Jim's cat!" Fraser suddenly realised what all the fuss had been about.

"Jet. Yes, he had rabies."

"He bit Jim's dad."

"I know. He went to hospital in Oban. They're giving him a course of injections. They think he'll be all right."

"You said people usually die."

"They do if they catch the disease, but you don't always get it even after you've been bitten. The doctors say Mr. Douglas will probably be OK, but they won't be really sure for a few more days. The only thing is…

"What?"

"It's almost as if he's got it already."

"How?"

"He's turned all nasty. He's started setting gins – you know steel traps that don't always kill the animals that get caught in them – and he goes out with his gun and shoots at everything he sees. It's as if he wants revenge on the animals for being bitten."

"Maybe he *has* caught it then," suggested Fraser. "So he'll die."

"I don't know. Even when people do get infected there's supposed to be a cure; that's why he's getting all those injections – only it doesn't always work. You see it's so long since there was any rabies in this country that nobody seems to know. Anyway, an inspector from the government has been to Kilrasken and disinfected the whole place. He's put up a notice to warn people that there's rabies about and he's made an 'Infected Area Order'. That means all the other cats have to be rounded up and put in quarantine. Misty and Tess have been vaccinated and have got to be muzzled and kept on the lead – just in case. And everybody's got to be specially careful about letting out their cats and dogs. That's why I didn't bring Sandy. I don't want to let him out any more than I have to."

Then Fraser told Rona what he had heard from One-eye.

"So the weasels are spreading it," muttered Rona. "I'll tell Cathy. Maybe there's something that could be done. In the meantime, if you see any animals behaving strangely around the garden don't go near them."

"I'm not supposed to go out at all."

"I know. But just in case. Don't take any chances."

"OK."

The next morning she was on the phone to him: "Fraser! Sandy slipped his lead last night and ran away. He's been out all night…" her voice broke down. "If you see him don't touch him. Don't talk to him. Keep away." She hung up.

THE AVENGER

Donald Douglas stalked the dry stubble of the autumn field, 12 bore, double barrelled shot gun under arm, like a god of vengeance.

The red weal on his hand itched a little and the hand felt warm; the weal in his mind burned like a branding iron and his brain blazed. At the far corner of the field, where the dry stone dyke was partly ruined and an animal trail ran across it, he had set a gin, a grim steel trap like the jaws of a bear. Today's victim was a rook, still flapping, trapped by one leg.

"Not worth a cartridge," he growled and broke the bird's neck with his heel.

One by one he checked and re-set his traps, killing any prisoners who were still alive and scouring the field for mild-eyed rabbits or hares which he would not bring home for the pot in case they were diseased. Then he headed for the wood where he could only hope to bring down pigeons or rooks which were not affected by rabies and which, away from nesting and lambing time, could not hurt him or his beasts in any way.

"They're all diseased," he muttered to himself, lighting a cigarette and kicking viciously at roots and stones and banks of dead leaves. Then he patrolled what he had made his beat for the last week since Jet had bitten him, firing off his gun at dry leaves dancing in a sudden gust of wind or bare branches groaning above his head as if all nature was possessed by rabies and he had a holy mission to cleanse and purify the countryside.

Fortunately he made so much noise stamping furiously along the dry, rustling trails and mumbling savagely to himself that the creatures of the woods were well able to keep out of his way.

Some of the bolder rooks knew that where there is a man with a gun there are sometimes wounded or dead animals to feast on. So a group of them followed him as they might have followed a tractor ploughing a field for the worms it turned up, or as gulls will follow a fishing boat at sea.

"Madness of the wolves," croaked one – the story had got about since One-eye had told Fraser and Fraser had asked Nephesh and the day birds of the gardens for news – "Do men have it too?"

"This one looks as if he has been bitten by a pack of weasels," said another.

"It was a cat," chipped in a third. "One of his own farm cats bit him. He turned the tame lightning on it and ever since he has been looking for some of us to kill in revenge."

"Idiot!" said the first bird, "Does he think he will ever catch anything with all that racket?"

A fat pigeon, crouching in cover, couldn't help chuckling to his mate, "When did you ever hear a rook noticing that someone else was noisy?"

Then, with a final curse and blast at nothing in particular, the man was off, out of the wood, on the path that led back to Kilrasken where he would sit all night by the fire and brood and stare at his swollen hand and think about his next painful injection at the hospital tomorrow.

FREEDOM

The cottage was empty; Fraser's mum had gone shopping.

The sky and the trees were empty too; empty of clouds and empty of leaves. Fraser had only been at the cottage in summer before and the sight of all those bare, twisted branches, like witches' fingers, was a little frightening.

On the ground everything was a bustle. The exceptionally cold, still, dry October weather had allowed the leaves to cling to the branches unusually late in the season, but now November's first frosts had nipped them and they lay, like piles of pheasants' feathers, in heaps everywhere, so that everything that moved, rustled. A tiny robin, turning leaves over in the hope of finding a juicy slug, made as much noise as a whole regiment of starlings; a squirrel scurrying back to his winter quarters with just one more acorn to add to his store sounded like the charge of a family of rabbits.

Fraser's trainers on the lawn crunched like the tell-tale footsteps of a giant. But this had to be the moment; so, with a guilty glance round the garden, he zipped up his leather jacket against the cold and rustled up the trail along which he had followed One-eye the morning he had rescued Barook from the trap.

If Sandy hadn't been seen, it could only be because he had gone to cover somewhere in the wood. If he didn't already know about the madness he must be warned and brought back home safely, if it wasn't already too late.

It was so cold as he crossed the field that each breath seemed to fill his lungs with ice, and yet when he breathed out, steam boiled from his mouth and nose. Fraser laughed. He felt like a dragon. He blew a cloud of steam in front of him and raced through it into the wood. If he could blow smoke like a dragon perhaps he could fly like a dragon. Like a great dragon in flight with powerful wing beats, breathing smoke in a cloud that shuts out the sun – hey! – watch out for those branches; dragons don't fly in woods – Klamath could have told you that.

Then the sickening thud of his head on hard ground.

No, he couldn't fly. Could he even walk?

Up slowly – easy does it – onto your knees first – there's a branch to hold on to. Funny how this cold makes you catch your breath. Take your time – that's better. Oh, oh! – the path's squirming underfoot; maybe better crawl a bit till you get your balance back. Rustle, rustle.

At least it was dry, otherwise his trousers would have been soaked by now.

One-eye's earth was near. Fraser wished he was small enough to wriggle down into its dark warmth and snuggle up to the fox, or that One-eye would suddenly appear to keep him company.

Or Sandy… if Sandy was still all right.

THE DRAGON'S EGG

Donald Douglas tramped the trail, enraged, following the bullet holes of his eyes, inviting – daring – something to move and show itself so that he could blast it and add it to the tally of his revenge. Three rooks perched, like little vultures, above his head, waiting for the worst – like vultures always hoping for the worst – clattering their dirty blunt beaks in anticipation, like a dog licking its lips.

There was a rustle.

"Show yourself, damn you!"

Then, at the corner of his eye – a flash of yellow – a big bounding body exploding towards him. He swung the gun and, point blank, without taking proper aim or even seeing what he was shooting at, gave it both barrels.

There was a yelp, a twisting of legs and tail in mid air, and the animal crashed off, howling, through the bushes.

Douglas rested his gun against a tree. It was the first thing he had hit for days.

"Serve it bloody right," he snarled. "Foxes, stray dogs – main carriers – need to destroy them all. That's one anyway."

He re-loaded the gun, lit a cigarette and stumbled off in vague pursuit of his victim, for he had enough reason and decency left in him to remember that if you wound an animal you are honour-bound to go after it and put it out of its misery.

The blackened match fell on a little brown leaf and bored a minute hole in it. From the hole there arose the tiniest smear of smoke and then a ragged orange rim glowed round the edge. Slowly the orange spread; slowly the smoke thickened and curled round a twist of yellow dry grass. A puff might have blown it out like a candle. But there was no-one to puff. Then one of the strands of grass turned orange; and then the smoke was orange – and there was flame and a crackling – and a curtain of fire leaped like a leopard upon the dusty dry grasses and leaves of the wood; and then, rising through the bushes, it roared like a leopard.

THE WEASELS

It was cold midday; One-eye was asleep; Barook was asleep. No friendly nose came to nuzzle Fraser. Only the cold. And the ground heaved and turned under him like a wild horse bucking its rider. Then he heard the voices; nasty angry little high pitched voices, quarrelling amongst themselves.

Then he saw the weasels.

Fraser had met weasels; little furry, snake-like killers with long claws like a small badger's and eye teeth like little daggers. He'd often seen their heads and bright eyes pop out of hedgerows inquisitively and he had often exchanged "What moves?" with them.

He knew they were active, intelligent little animals, curious about everything and courageous beyond the bounds of common sense. He had heard how they would kill rabbits several times larger than themselves, face up to cats and even dogs and fight furiously even when gripped by the unrelenting talons of Kievarr the kestrel or Nephesh.

He rather admired them for their courage and their cunning, but he knew also that they were the most ruthless killers in the woods, quite without fear when the bloodlust was on them, so that much bigger animals like One-eye and Barook preferred to give them a wide berth.

Today there were three of them, quarrelling and snarling in their high, harsh voices and Fraser noticed flecks of foam at their mouths. He tried to stand, but fell back onto his knees.

Weasels usually disappeared very quickly when confronted by humans so that he had never exchanged more than a greeting with any he had met before. But these three made no attempt to run.

"Look what we've got here," said the foremost, nervously licking his lips.

"Fancy some blood?" snapped a second.

"Easy now boys, what moves?" Fraser called, on hands and knees but still looming over the little animals.

"What moves, he asks," sneered the first weasel. "He thinks he can talk like us. We move, cub. And we'll soon move you. When we move everybody moves.

"We are the weasels, the weasels!"

The other two took up the chant, "The weasels, the weasels."

Fraser saw their shifty eyes, long claws and slavering jaws and got ready to take the bites that he knew must come on the padded leather of his jacket for he realised that if these dripping teeth so much as scratched his skin he would be in danger of the same madness that Jim's dad was perhaps even now living through.

And then from nowhere came a streak of red fur, a swift snapping of jaws and two of the weasels were tossed, skulls cracked like egg shells, over One-eye's shoulder. The third, totally fearless in his madness, leaped and sank his teeth in the fox's muzzle. Another shake and bite and the demented beast was dead.

But blood spurted through the red fur from tiny pinpricks on the fox's face. One-eye knew that his long warrior's life was near its end and his history of narrow escapes was over, for it was part of the ancient wisdom of the foxes that a bite on the face from a rabid animal is almost always fatal.

"One-eye!" screamed Fraser.

The fox shook himself and rubbed a paw over his nose as though to wipe away the poison.

"It's nothing. I have come away alive after real bites from dogs. How should a jag like this hurt me?"

But his ears were flattened against his head and the droop of his tail told Fraser that he knew better.

"I will go away till the wound has healed," he added and with a quick turn disappeared into the bushes.

Fraser called, "One-eye! Come back! Men can cure this."

But the dry bushes and rustling leaves were, for once, quite silent. Then from across the burn came a last call, then a crash and a rustle and the wood was still again.

THE RED DRAGON

All animals fear "The Red Dragon" as they call fire.

It can outrun the swiftest runner; its smoke can outfly all but the greatest of birds. Only those who live in water can easily escape its roar and chase. It is hatched out of the smallest of eggs and yet, if properly fed, it can grow taller than the tallest tree.

When Donald Douglas strode off in pursuit of whatever it was he had shot he left behind, unnoticed, a fledgling fire that could scarcely crawl. But it soon found wings and, riding easily in a light east wind off the moor, began to spread through the wood, downstream from Kwarutta's pool.

Like a roaring curtain it advanced, crackling the dry leaves and twisted fibres of the undergrowth. Before it fled a small army of mice and voles and squirrels wakened from their light winter sleep. Those who could, took to the water and swam downstream to where Sebek, the pike, waited to welcome them in his pool at the foot of the wood. Above, a cloud of rooks and pigeons and starlings rose and fled from the suffocating smoke. Douglas turned back. The thing he had shot was well away, or perhaps had gone to cover somewhere, in which case it was probably already dead.

He caught the sharp stink of smoke and stopped. Then he heard the crackling and saw the face of the fire advancing upon him.

For a moment he thought he was trapped and the sweat broke out on his forehead. Then, realising that the wind was weak and the fire was moving slowly, he turned away from its path and began a long detour which would take him back to Kilrasken.

"That'll burn the devils out," he chuckled.

Lower down the wood and much further away, Fraser, on hands and knees, also picked up the faint smell of fire – but he had other things to think of – the grinning jaws of the weasels; One-eye bounding off after his last kill. Meanwhile, under his knees and below the palms of his hands the ground heaved and turned as if it was alive and was trying to throw him off balance.

But then came wisps of charred grass and little specs of ash floating on the light wind; and later the sound of crackling.

Slowly it dawned on Fraser that the wood was burning and that he lay in the path of the fire. He struggled to his feet – and fell. He gritted his teeth and turned on hands and knees to face the slow crawl along the bucking trail to the edge of the wood and safety. But all the time he crawled he seemed to be swamped by the heaving of the ground like a small boat in a heavy sea. The flecks of ash were falling more thickly now and the smoke was beginning to sting his eyes, but still his head would not clear and the ground would not stay still under his feet to let him get away. What was the use? What if the soft smoke came and soothed him to sleep? The ground heaved less violently when he didn't try to move, so that it rocked him into a pleasant kind of dream, with no weasels and One-eye there beside him.

Fraser jerked awake as a wet, blunt nose rooted into his face and a gruff voice he recognised at once grunted in his ear.

"Boy with our tongue! This is no time for sleep."

Barook the badger, alerted by the smell of smoke filtering

down into his earth, had scrambled to the surface and was making off to safety at a surprising speed when he saw the boy.

"I can't move, Barook," gasped Fraser.

"You must move," snapped the badger and he nudged the boy again. "Up now, on four legs like we do." It was not so long since Barook had fathered a litter and the instinct to push reluctant cubs out into the world to fend for themselves was still strong.

Fraser tried again and made a little distance down the trail.

"Keep moving," growled the badger. "The Dragon is behind us. Can you not feel his breath?"

Fraser could. The roar of the fire was loud now and the heat was falling in waves as the wind shifted direction.

He struggled on, sometimes crawling on hands and knees, sometimes standing up and steadying himself with his hands on the trunks of trees or clutching armfuls of rhododendron bush. Whenever he stumbled, there was Barook to grunt a hoarse encouragement, "Keep moving. The Dragon is behind us."

But by now more persuasive than anything the badger could say was the roaring of the fire as it shrivelled the undergrowth and licked hungrily around the trunks of the biggest trees. And the heat! Fraser's hands were sticky with sweat and salty rivulets ran down his forehead and stung his eyes.

Then there was the wall; he was over it; he rolled in the short, crisp grass of the field; and then he slept because he knew he was safe.

He didn't hear or feel as the fire blazed its way through the wood over Sebek's pool till it stopped, baffled, at the edge of the wetlands where even after a hard dry October there were still pools and puddles and soft spongy places.

104

There it danced and raged and shook its claws at the loch beyond, until gradually, like an exhausted giant, it collapsed grumbling on the heaps of filthy black ash with which it had smothered the dens and nests and burrows of the people of the wood.

SANDY

Fraser wakened, shivering in the evening chill, with the sound of barking in his ears.

Just barking.

Then the wet lick of a dog's tongue and he opened his eyes to see Sandy, covered in dirt, standing over him.

Sandy talked! What a tale he had to tell – of the stinging lash of the tame lightning; of being chased by the Red Dragon; of getting lost and not being able to track his way back home because of the fire; of how he had wandered round in the wetlands – like all labradors he loved water – and he had found Fraser and he was delighted to see him, but his leg was sore.

All this and a lot more Sandy related as he poured out his adventures to Fraser – but the boy heard only barking.

He struggled to his feet and found, to his surprise, that the ground stayed still under him. He could see that the dog was limping and that there was blood on his leg. It meant life or death to Sandy, and possibly to Fraser, for him to know if the wound had come from the bite of a rabid animal, but, just when he needed his gift of tongues most, it had deserted him.

He saw also the look of puzzlement and disappointment in the big brown eyes when he didn't answer the dog in his own tongue.

He did the next best thing.

"Come on Sandy," he said in human speech. And together, sick boy and wounded dog, they limped across the fields to the houses of Dunadd.

REMISSION

The consultant turned to Fraser's mum and dad as they sat round his bed. "He's back to normal. It's something we call 'Spontaneous Remission'. That just means that his condition has improved of its own accord. We don't know why, and of course he could deteriorate again at any time. Fraser will always have to be very careful and take his medicine regularly. Meanwhile, there's no reason why he shouldn't get out and about – get a lot of fresh air – and come and see me again in a fortnight."

Fraser's first visit was to Rona to see how Sandy was. The labrador demonstrated this for himself as he bounded up excitedly, though he still seemed puzzled that Fraser only talked to him in human speech.

"You can never really tell what's going on in humans' minds," thought the dog.

Rona explained, "No, it wasn't a bite. He had three shot gun pellets in his left hind leg. He was lucky just to be winged by the shot. He's OK."

"Was it Jim's dad that shot him?"

Rona shrugged, "Nobody saw it. It could have been anybody."

"Dirty rat. I hope he dies."

"Fraser, he's sick. He may be dying. It's like Jet and the weasels; its not their fault."

"Then he's the one who should be shot – like Jet was."

"But he might get better. The other cats are all right. They've been allowed back to the farm and there's been no other cases reported. The inspector's cancelled the 'Infected Area Order,' so that means he thinks there's no other animals left with rabies. It looks like the fire killed off all the sick animals."

"How did it all start anyway?"

"Cathy says there haven't been any cases in Britain for years, so she thinks somebody must have smuggled a sick animal in from abroad – you know they're all supposed to go into quarantine for six months to make sure they're all right, unless they have a special pet passport."

"I suppose we'll never really know."

"Main thing is the bad dream's over." Rona fondled Sandy's ears.

The next day Jim's mum phoned the cottage.

"How's Fraser ? Heard he was a lot better. Would he like to spend a few days at the farm?"

Fraser's mum was doubtful. "Are you sure it will be all right? How's Donald?"

Mrs Douglas let herself go. "We've just had news from the hospital that he's clear. We're so relieved. He's been lucky. He didn't contract the – thing – the illness." She couldn't bring herself to pronounce the dreaded word 'rabies'.

"He thought he was going to die, you know. He started acting so strangely that I wondered if, maybe, he *had* got it. But it was just the worry, or maybe just a very mild dose."

The possibility that she and her young son might have lived under the same roof as a man who was rabid and murderous, even if only for a few days until those awful, painful injections had overcome the poison, was too terrible for her to think about.

"Anyway he's his old self again."

And so he was. The cats were back in the barn and Misty

and Tess were off on the moors, bringing down the last of the sheep for the winter.

"Thought the Old Man was going to snuff it," confided Jim as if he had known all along about rabies and the danger his dad had been in. "Was worried it might get into the beasts (he meant the cattle and sheep) and they'd all have to be slaughtered. Cost a lot of money, that would. Mind you, I know what started it."

"What?" asked Fraser.

"Mind yon funny dog? That started it."

"Where did it come from?"

Jim was deflated. He hadn't thought as far as that.

"Oh somewhere. Glasgow, maybe."

On his way back to the cottage Fraser saw Klamath flying overhead on a visit to one of his favourite pools on the moor and he remembered what the bird had told him about an animal being thrown into the water from that strange white ship in the loch.

"Not a ghost ship after all," he said to himself. "More a ship of the plague."

THE PIT

FEARGAL THE WANDERER

None of this would have happened if One-eye had come back. Legends tell of an old fox with one eye who had survived the most terrible thing that can happen to a wild animal, hunting among the black peat hags of Rannoch Moor. But he was not seen again around Dunadd.

No hunting territory is without a fox for long, however, and when the winter frosts hardened the ground and game grew scarce a new claimant appeared on the scene. Feargal was not much more than a cub; a young hunter in his first year, he had still to mate. He came one evening in January, snuffling up the hillside from somewhere to the north, and found the old trail that had been used by One-eye and his ancestors. There was no smell or track of fox so he pushed on hungrily in search of a territory he could mark out as his own. Deep in the wood he came on the main entrance to Barook's network of tunnels which the badger had shared with One-eye for years.

Barook had recently completed the winter clean-out of his set. He had dragged out all his old bedding and collected fresh bracken and dry leaves and brought them underground to line his sleeping quarters. Now that he had no fox to share with, his set was cleaner and fresher than it had ever been before and Barook grunted with pleasure as he surveyed it.

Up at the entrance Feargal also grunted with pleasure. This looked like an ideal home for a young fox with nowhere to go and his nose told him that there was no rival living there. He could see the signs of a badger's occupation, but he had met badgers before and knew that they were usually prepared to share their quarters with foxes. So he crawled confidently down Barook's main tunnel.

The badger had just wakened up and was enjoying a good scratch before clambering out for his night's hunting. He stopped at once when he heard the movement above and then caught the sharp stink of fox.

"What moves?" he growled.

"Feargal the wanderer," was the reply. By this Feargal meant that he had no permanent lair or territory of his own and slept each day in a different place in whatever cover he could find.

"There's no room here," snapped Barook.

"I'm sure such a mighty digger as yourself would not grudge a homeless fox a corner in your set."

Badgers are easy-going by nature and at one time Barook would have made no objection, just as his father had not objected many years ago when One-eye had arrived as a young fox at the mouth of the set. But in the months since One-eye had disappeared Barook had got used to living in quarters that did not smell of fox and now with his winter clean-out just completed he was in no mood to entertain another strongly-smelling guest.

"Get out," he snarled, shuffling forward on powerfully armed paws.

Feargal backed up the tunnel growling, for he knew that no animal is a match for a badger underground.

When he was clear he barked, "May your hide rot in your miserable rabbit warren, flat foot, slug eater... " and Feargal added all the insults he could think of on the spur of the moment. Then he went off to hunt down wind, well away from the angry badger. He skirted the blackened area where the previous year's great fire had raged and his night's work took him round by the edge of the wood and over the crumbling boundary wall which separated it from the moor.

By this time the sky in the east was turning from black to greenish grey in the first glimmerings of the dawn, so that the dark cliffs of Sgurr Mor stood out against it. So the fox was glad to find, in the middle of a thicket of bracken, the entrance to a long abandoned rabbit warren which, with a little digging and scraping, he was able to enlarge enough to give him shelter for the day.

Here Feargal decided to stay; there was no other fox in the territory and the hunting was as good as any he could expect to find at this time of year; besides ,the old warren could be enlarged with a bit of scraping to give him all the shelter he would need.

AN EARTH FIT FOR CUBS

One evening, about a month after he moved in, Feargal had a visitor.

He was standing at the mouth of the earth sniffing the night air and was just about to trot off to begin his night's hunting when there was a rustle in the bracken.

"What moves?" he barked.

"Sionnaidh* the wanderer," was the reply and a small vixen stepped out onto the trail. "Who are you?"

"Feargal on his own," said Feargal to show that he did not have a mate and that it was safe for her to come closer.

She stepped forward shyly. "Is the hunting good here?"

"The hunting is never good in the Dead Time," grumbled Feargal. "But it's better here than in most places," he added quickly because he didn't want her to go away.

She crept closer and they sniffed each other's scents with approval. That night they hunted together and in the dawn Sionnaidh curled up beside Feargal in a corner of the old warren.

In the twilight of the next evening, before going out to hunt, they danced the heather dance together, on hind legs, paws on each other's shoulders, in front of the entrance to the warren.

After that night's hunting Sionnaidh said, "I will hunt with you if you will let me and I will bear your cubs, but first

*Pronounced Shoanay

we must make this wretched hole into an earth fit for cubs to be born in."

Feargal was as lazy as any dog fox and he was quite happy with his lair as it was, although he had to admit it was not up to the standard of Barook's set, or even of the earth he had been born in. But he didn't want to quarrel with Sionnaidh; so he simply said, "Yes darling," and agreed to help her excavate a palace for their litter when it arrived.

For the next few days Sionnaidh scrabbled and scraped; her forepaws cut trenches through the clean earth and her hind legs drove the loose soil back out of the tunnel in great scoops.

Feargal looked on approvingly and gave a little advice now and again when he thought it was needed: "Darling, a little bit to the left and you'll miss that big boulder." But he was really dying to roam after rabbits under the stars.

Sionnaidh dug for herself and her unborn cubs. She knew that if she had to depend on Feargal to make a home for their family she might as well give birth in a field like Ardair the hare. At last the earth was complete. Feargal surveyed his mate's work with pride, as though he had done the whole thing himself.

Only on the south where the ground rose towards a small hillock, were the arrangements unsatisfactory. Here Sionnaidh's tunnels ran into a jumble of boulders. At first she tried to dig round them and excavated a lot of loose pebbles, but eventually she was stopped by the bigger stones, great square boulders past which she couldn't dig, and the new earth had to stop there without that extra passage to the surface which most foxes prefer to have for safety.

Outside the entrance, among the stiff stalks of the bracken, the spoil from the digging lay in loose heaps. Anxious not to attract attention to the opening, Sionnaidh scuffed these further away so that the loose stuff was spread out over the Goat Trail; fine soil and loose chips and gravel, and among them a stone different from the rest because when it fell out onto the open track it shone in the sunlight.

THE RING

Fraser wasn't sure that he wanted to spend his Easter holiday at the cottage. One-eye would not be there – but even if by some miracle he had returned Fraser would not be able to speak to him, and without his gift of voices he felt like a stranger in Dunadd.

On the other hand he was looking forward to seeing Jim Douglas again and Rona, and this almost made him forget about having lost his animal voices.

He was soon reminded.

Outside his bedroom window there was a tall sycamore tree and in its branches, at about eye level with the upstairs windows of the house, a pair of magpies were building their nest. Fraser could see them regularly coming and going with sticks and twiglets in their beaks. Occasionally on these journeys the magpies were chased by larger birds, rooks or gulls.

All Fraser could hear when this happened were caws and chirrups, but he knew from past experience that, although they sometimes could pass on useful information, the conversation of garden birds was not usually very interesting.

Then one day the hen magpie, chased closely by a rook, dropped something hard which clinked when it fell onto the roof tiles and rolled down into the gutter. The rook checked itself in its flight, took a quick look at what the magpie had been carrying and then showed no further interest.

Fraser could see it from his window, lying there glinting

just out of reach. He ran downstairs and came back with a long-handled broom. With this he was just able to reach the thing and push it out of the gutter so that it fell onto the lawn in the garden below.

He ran down at once and searched feverishly until he found it. When he picked it up he saw that it was a ring; not an ordinary ring but one with a curious spiral twist running all round it; he cupped it in his hand and found that, for its size, it was surprisingly heavy. Fraser slipped it in his pocket and it was then that he wished he could have his voice back so that he could ask the magpie where she had found it.

He didn't mention the ring to Jim Douglas when he visited him the next day at Kilrasken farm. Jim tended to scoff at things like that as "girls' toys."

But he did show it to Rona when he met her walking Sandy a few days later. After the usual welcome from the dog he reached into his pocket:

"Rona, have you seen anything like this before?"

Rona took the ring, held it between her finger and thumb and looked at it closely. Then she slipped it on her finger, but it was too big. Finally she weighed it in the palm of her hand.

"It must be gold. Feel the weight of it," she said, handing it back to him. "Where did you get it?"

Fraser told her.

"Magpies often steal things and hide them in their nests," she said. "Somebody must have lost it. It's a pity… " she broke off.

"It's a pity," Fraser continued for her, "that I can't ask the magpie where she got it."

"Yes, but it's much more important that you stay well. Remember what you promised about the pills. You're not going to do anything stupid, are you?"

"No, it's OK. I'm not going to stop taking them just because somebody's lost a stupid ring."

"You'll have to hand it in at the police station. After all, it's gold and it might be valuable. It's very unusual," she added. "I've never seen one like it."

They went together to the police station and the officer on duty took down all the details and gave Fraser a receipt.

"If anybody claims it they'll probably get in touch with you. There could be a reward if it's really gold. If you don't hear anything come back in six months; if it hasn't been claimed you get it to keep."

That night a storm struck Dunadd. As the thunder rolled and rumbled around the house Fraser could feel the crashes shaking his mind; shaking, shaking! And as the lightning darted in the dark outside he felt as though spears of fire were darting inside his head.

Eventually he fell asleep, still shaking.

When he wakened the thunder had stopped; outside there was a strange stillness as the ground soaked up the heavy rain that had fallen during the storm.

Then he heard the cry, "A kill; a mouse," as Nephesh called to his mate.

THERE COULD BE CLUES

Over the next few days Fraser had two important conversations.

The first, which he did not fully understand, was with the consultant, who called to see him at the cottage. What really mattered was what the consultant said, not to Fraser himself, but to his mum and dad outside his bedroom door when they thought he wasn't listening.

"It's alarming that there should have been a recurrence so soon. Last attack was October, wasn't it?" He paused. "There is a new drug I'm going to put him on, but I have to be quite frank with you; there is no guarantee that it will work."

"What if it doesn't?" asked Fraser's dad.

They must have heard him turning in bed because the consultant lowered his voice so that Fraser couldn't hear what he said; but he thought he could hear his mum let out a gasp, "Oh no."

Vaguely Fraser felt he should be worried, but everything seemed so much like a dream that he decided he would simply follow wherever the dream led him.

That meant he had to talk to the magpie. As soon as his parents had seen the consultant out he got up and tiptoed shakily to his bedroom window, opened it and whistled across to the bird who was sitting on six bluish green eggs she had just laid in the nest.

"What moves?"

"My eggs are warm. The chicks will be hatching soon."

"You dropped something on my roof the other day."

"What was that?"

Fraser found this difficult to answer for there are no words for "ring" or "gold" in bird talk. "Something like a coiled up centipede. It was hard and shiny."

"A snail?" suggested the magpie.

"No. You couldn't eat it."

"Don't remember."

"Please try. You were being chased by one of the rooks."

"Now I do remember something nice and shiny. I'd forgotten about it."

"Where did you find it?"

"Don't remember."

"You must remember. It's important."

"I've completely forgotten." She fluttered her wings to emphasise how complete her forgetfulness was and then went off into a song about how beautiful her chicks were going to be.

As so often before, Fraser was infuriated by the silliness of garden birds, but the hen was only interested in hatching her brood and there was no chance of getting any more out of her. In desperation he turned to his old friend Klamath who was flying on one of his patrols to the lochans on the moor.

"A bright shiny thing like a coiled centipede. No good to eat," repeated the heron to make sure he had understood the question, for he didn't see the point of looking for anything of that sort. "I can't see things like that myself when I'm in flight, but I'll ask Eye of the Wind when I'm up on the moor and if it was on lower ground Kievarr the kestrel would be the most likely bird to see it."

Two days later Klamath was back from his fishing expedition on the moor.

"Beyond the wood," he honked, landing on the roof of the garage from which he could see Fraser at his window.

"On the Goat Trail where it passes a heap of big boulders. Kievarr says he saw it. He dropped down to hover for a closer look but it was no good to eat. Good fishing!" and the big bird launched himself into the air and flapped off to try his luck on the wetlands by the shore of the loch.

Fraser knew the spot.

About a quarter of a mile from the ledge where Dyer's caravan had stood, the Goat Trail skirts the boundary wall of the wood for a short distance before starting to climb the steep, bracken-covered slopes that led on to the moor. At one point a jumble of boulders, partly overgrown by ferns and moor grass blocks the way and the trail twists sharply to the left to avoid it. This must have been where the magpie had seen the glittering object and, although it was no use to her either for eating or nest building, she had taken it simply because its shiny gleam caught her eye.

Neither Fraser, Klamath nor Kievarr could understand this, but Rona did at once when Fraser talked to her about it again.

"It's a beautiful thing; that's why she took it," she explained. "I'd love to have it myself. You boys are so thick. You're not interested in anything you can't eat. You're just like Sandy."

"You're just like a magpie," he laughed. "You've got no more brains."

"Well, it would be nice if you helped to find its owner. Somebody's probably desperate to get it back."

"Well now I know where the magpie found it."

"How do you know that?" Rona was immediately suspicious.

"Klamath told me."

"Have you stopped taking your medicine?"

"No!"

"Then how do you know what Klamath said?"

"The thunderstorm last week. My voices came back then."

"Oh!" Rona realised how serious this might be for Fraser.

"What I don't understand is who could have dropped it on the Goat Trail? Nobody lives there," he went on.

"Hill walkers sometimes go up that way to climb the Sgurr."

"But why would they take off a ring in the middle of a hill walk?"

"I don't know."

"If I wasn't sick I'd go and have a look for myself; there might be clues; bloodstains; maybe a weapon. There's probably been a murder."

"Have you been reading too many detective stories?"

"There might be footprints at least. I wish I could go."

"You mean you want me to go and have a look for you?"

"Do you think you should go on your own?" said Fraser, concerned.

"I'll take Sandy with me; he might just sniff out something interesting."

THE KING MUST GO

Kids were born to the nanny goats in April. Bhuiridh watched over them protectively. But his hold on the herd was growing weaker. In the rut the previous autumn Gobhar had at last dared to push his rivalry as far as a head-to-head challenge.

With lowered brows and swinging horns the two bucks had faced each other and the thud of skull against skull, the clank and rattle of locked horns wrestling, had drawn gasps of admiration from the watching females and younger males. For long minutes they had butted, battered and wrestled until Bhuiridh sensed that his strength was ebbing and that the younger buck would sooner or later wear him down. He called up all his reserves of energy and cunning and, remembering an old trick he had learned early in his career as a fighter, slipped to one side, caught his opponent off balance, struck him square in the ribs with the full force of his battering-ram head and knocked him to the ground, winded and at the mercy of Bhuiridh's hooves and horns.

Gobhar had slunk away, ashamed and nursing that special kind of hatred that grows out of humiliation, and swore revenge.

Bhuiridh had pranced away, horns held high, as he had done so often before, following a fight, but this time he knew he was only acting a part. He realised that he was no longer the strongest buck in the herd, and he was thinking of the day when he would be defeated, deposed and humiliated himself before his wives, children and grandchildren as he had deposed and humiliated his predecessor.

Now, in April, there were newborn kids again and the nannies were fussing over them. This was the only time of real danger for the herd, for no predator could tackle a full-grown goat. But the stumbling, tumbling kids – by day Eye of the Wind and by night Cruach the cat or the foxes would steal them away for a prize feast.

Guardianship of the herd was more important at this time than ever. Bhuiridh still did his job well. There was no slackening in his watchfulness, but one night Feargal, hunting for his mate who was about to give birth to their litter, took one of the kids.

Gobhar took advantage of the situation.

"Can't handle a fox any more, can you? Think you could still see off a stoat? If Cruach came for a kid in the night you'd sleep right through it, wouldn't you? Don't you think it's time to step down and leave the herd to somebody who can look after it?"

Bhuiridh bristled and automatically lowered his horns in the well-rehearsed guard position from which he had won so many battles before.

Their heads clashed; the crack of skulls sounded over the moor and echoed into the wood so that the message went out to all who could hear that a contest for the lordship of the entire territory was taking place. The smaller creatures hid, as children shelter from a thunderstorm.

The larger predators, Cruach and the foxes, took note that there might soon be a new guardian of the herd and far off in the depth of the wood Barook stayed awake specially to listen to the news of the great fight. In the sky Eye of the Wind and Kievarr watched with interest and the gulls and rooks and jackdaws passed the news from treetop to treetop down into the gardens of Dunadd until at last a robin hopping from one hawthorn bush to another cheeped to a chaffinch across the hedge the epic news that Bhuiridh, chief of the goats of the moor, had been battered and beaten, and had slunk away from the herd to brood on his defeat, all alone.

* * *

Rona went to the Goat Trail with Sandy as she had promised. She skirted the wood, crossed the Ballagan Burn on stepping stones and turned along the track towards the great tangle of boulders where the ring had been found.

Here she met the new king. Hooves foursquare, head lowered, horns swinging, stood Gobhar with the nannies and the kids behind him. It was the first test of his leadership and he had to prove himself.

Rona stopped short on the trail and hauled Sandy in by the lead.

The dog challenged the goat, "Give way! Clear out or I'll tear you to pieces!" But he knew he was on the lead and his challenge was really only meant to impress his mistress.

There was no bluff about Gobhar. He lowered his head further and swung his horns like twin scimitars. "Get off my ground or I'll kick you off the moor."

He pawed the ground as a sure sign that he was about to charge.

Rona was not afraid of animals and she had often helped Cathy to treat sheep and goats and even much bigger beasts like cattle and horses, but she knew that with the kids behind him Gobhar meant business and it was safer not to provoke him. So she shortened her grip on Sandy's lead and dragged him away.

The dog followed unwillingly, barking the most blood-chilling threats over his shoulder. "Lucky for you I can't get at you. I'd tear your throat out and..."

Gobhar turned away, his first test triumphantly passed, and began to graze while the herd looked on in approval.

THE SKULL

In the new earth four fox cubs were born; little blind, greyish bundles. Sionnaidh waited until they were a month old and could scramble about and then gently nuzzled them up the entrance passage of the earth until they spilled out into the great big world beyond.

At first they were too timid to stray far from the mouth of the earth, but they soon grew bolder and in a few weeks were foraging in wider and wider circles in the bracken and among the boulders, on the moor and in the wood.

They sprawled and wrestled with each other aimlessly at first, but more and more they played at hunting and killing. One of them would stalk a tuft of grass or a sprig of heather and then suddenly pounce and sink his teeth in an imaginary rabbit or rat. Another would find an old bone or a stick and worry it to death. Then two of them would seize opposite ends of the same stick and wrestle over it until a third jumped on the pair of them and all three would collapse in a tumbling heap, the stick forgotten.

Later they explored further afield, along the wall of the wood to the place where the Ballagan Burn splashed down from the moor. This greatly excited them for the cubs had never seen a rushing burn before. What was this long, silvery creature which rushed and rushed and yet never seemed to go anywhere? At first they stood off, barking and growling, but when the burn paid no attention to them they crept closer and dared to touch it with an exploring paw. The strange sensation of wetness made them jump back in surprise, but soon their confidence returned and they came to accept the burn as something as natural as the bracken and the boulders. Then they followed it into the wood as far as Kwarutta's pool where they wasted a great deal of energy dashing into the water after moorhens.

In the opposite direction the boulders behind the earth were a special playground for the cubs; a kind of gymnasium of steep rocks for them to clamber over and narrow spaces they could crawl into. There were big dark hollow holes under the stones where they could play hide and seek, but they never stayed there long for there was a strange, mouldy smell about the place quite unlike the clean air of the earth.

One evening the oldest and boldest of the cubs found a treasure there. He had great difficulty in getting it out for it was bigger than he was, but he tugged and hauled and heaved and shook it, growling all the time deep in his throat. Then it stuck between two big stones and the cub gave up and went off to play with the others.

But the next night he came back again, digging and scraping until eventually he found a way of getting it out into the open. One final heave and it came away. The cub sat down suddenly on his tail and the thing rolled off down the slope until it stopped against some dense bracken on the opposite side of the Goat Trail.

Then he barked to draw the attention of the others, "Look what I've found. I caught it all by myself," and he licked it and gnawed at it.

When Feargal heard the cries he trotted over out of curiosity to see what his eldest son had found and there, eyeless and jawless, pale and cold, was a smooth, round skull.

VANISHING EVIDENCE

Fraser did not get any better.

The consultant visited him regularly and seemed concerned that the new drug he had prescribed didn't seem to be having any effect. Fraser didn't pay much attention to what he said, but he did notice that his mum never seemed to smile any more.

He could hardly crawl out of his bed some mornings and his only interest was in the tales of the animals of the wood and moor which he got from the birds. For those who hunted by night his main source of information was Nephesh. Fraser didn't sleep well these nights and often he would get up when his mum and dad were asleep, open his window and call softly, "Nephesh, what moves?"

If the owl was within hearing distance he would come and perch on a chimney pot and call back, "Nothing moves, Birdboy" – this was a name he had given Fraser – and then he would tell of his night's hunting or pass on news of Barook. It was Nephesh who assured Fraser that One-eye had not come back.

By day most of Fraser's information came from Klamath. New people had moved into a house down the road and they had dug a large ornamental pond in their back garden and stocked it with goldfish. To their great annoyance Klamath had discovered this and made a point of dropping in regularly for a snack.

The heron covered a lot of ground in his flights from pool to pool and he knew more of what went on by day than anyone except Eye of the Wind. It was Klamath who gave Fraser one last hope that One-eye might still be alive.

"I heard a story from some of the geese coming south last autumn, of a fox with one eye hunting somewhere on the moors to the north," he said.

Fraser told Klamath how the leader of the goats had stopped Rona and Sandy from exploring the spot where the ring had been found, so when Gobhar took the herd up the Goat Trail as Bhuiridh had done so often, and settled them in their other grazing grounds on the moor, the heron made a special visit to the garden to tell him that the goats were gone.

Fraser told Rona and made her promise to go back now that the way was clear to try to solve the mystery of the gold ring.

She went on her next day off and that night came to visit Fraser with a story so strange that it almost made him forget that he was ill.

"I went the same way as last time and was just past the place where the goat stopped us. I had Sandy on the extending lead and he was trotting on ahead when he stopped suddenly and started barking at something on the track. You'll never guess what it was." She paused and waited for Fraser to ask. "A skull! A human skull! It just lay there as if it was looking at me out of those big, hollow eyes."

"What did you do?" gasped Fraser. "Have you got it with you?"

"I ran away," she said.

"Ran away!" Fraser was disgusted.

"It was horrible. So I went to the police station and a policewoman came back with me, but when we got there it was gone.

"Are you sure this is the place?" she asked.

"I said, 'Yes,' but I don't think she believed me."

"I want to speak to Sandy," demanded Fraser.

When the dog had been fetched and had got over his surprise that Fraser could talk to him in his own language again, the boy began to question him.

"Did you find anything interesting today?"

"Not really. There was an old skull on the Goat Trail but there was no meat on it and it didn't smell good. I think it was old, very old."

"What did it smell like?"

"Sort of mouldy, as if it had been lying in the mud for ages. Also," Sandy wrinkled his nose in disgust, "there was a stink of fox about it." Like most dogs Sandy despised foxes almost as much as he disliked cats.

"Fox!" Fraser would have put his ears up if he had been a dog. "You sure it was fox?"

"How can you possibly mistake the stink of a fox?" Sandy snorted. "I'd have thought that even a human could recognise fox scent."

"One-eye," muttered Fraser. "Has he come back at last?"

"How should I know? One fox is as bad as another as far as I'm concerned."

That night Nephesh went hunting over another part of his territory so that Fraser didn't get the chance to ask him if he had any news of One-eye. As he lay in bed unable to sleep and uninterested in the chatter of the bats outside, Fraser decided that, sick or not, he must go to the Goat Trail to see for himself.

ON THE TRACK
OF THE SKULL

It was late one warm May afternoon when Fraser struggled into his outdoor clothes and slipped away along the track that led across the fields into the wood and past Barook's set. This time he had further to go because the Goat Trail ran along the far side of the wood, but he reckoned he had several hours before his parents came home and he would be missed.

There was a lump in his throat as he passed One-eye's old hunting grounds, but he pressed on as fast as he could. Barook would be fast asleep at that time of day anyway. He crossed the Ballagan Burn, now fresh and clean again, and then, to save time, cut across the dead part of the wood where last year's great fire had swept through it. The fresh green growth of spring was coming up but there were blackened bushes and charred tree trunks everywhere. His feet kicked up puffs of black ash and there was a smell of soot in the air.

Fraser was glad when he was across that dark scar in the wood and could follow the boundary wall till he came to a place where it was easy to climb.

"If I was well I could climb it at any place," he thought to himself.

Then he was on the Goat Trail, and he doubled back in the direction of the wild tangle of boulders near where, according to what Klamath and Rona had said, both the ring and the skull had been found.

Although it was still several hours before sunset, the cubs were outside the earth playing. They dropped out of sight as soon as they picked up the boy's scent.

Whatever Sandy thought about the smell of fox, humans have such poor noses that they can't detect it at a distance and Fraser would never have known the cubs were there if they had behaved like sensible foxes and kept quiet or if Sionnaidh or Feargal had been there to keep them in order. But they were only cubs on their own and before long, although they did have enough sense to keep out of sight, they were tumbling over each other in the bracken and making a great deal of noise.

"Got you."

"No you didn't."

"I'm faster than you."

"I've got the skull."

Fraser heard their sharp barks and stopped. Foxes they were, but not One-eye.

"Hiya kids," he called. "What moves?"

The cubs froze.

"Who was that?" asked the oldest and boldest, the one who had found the skull and was now sitting on it.

"There's nobody there," said number two cub. "Only that stupid human."

"I heard that," said Fraser with a chuckle. "I'm a human all right, but I'm not as stupid as you think. I know you've got the skull."

The cubs were petrified. Unfortunately this strange being was between them and the only entrance to the earth or they would have bolted underground.

"We didn't know it was your skull," whimpered the oldest and boldest. "We'll give it back if you want."

Fraser was just about to explain that it wasn't his skull but that he would like to see it when there was a snarl behind

135

him and a blurr of red shot past and crouched between him and the cubs, every tooth bared to the gums.

It was Sionnaidh.

"Keep back," she snarled. And then to the cubs, "Run! Keep under cover. I'll call when it's safe to come back." How she regretted not having been able to dig another entrance at the back of the earth.

"Keep back," she repeated, the bristles on the back of her neck standing up as stiff as a brush.

Fraser could hear scufflings in the undergrowth behind her. He sat down.

"I'm a friend of foxes," he explained. "I came looking for my friend One-eye. He saved my life once. Have you seen him?"

Sionnaidh was suspicious. The idea of a man with a beast's tongue who said his life had been saved by a fox was new to her and she had never heard of One-eye.

"You haven't a dog with you?" she asked.

"No. Nor tame lightning either."

"What do you want?"

"I'm looking for One-eye. He's an old fox and he has been ill. You haven't seen him?"

"I don't know anything about him." She was still suspicious, but there was something in the tone of the boy's voice as he asked after his friend that made her feel that he was telling the truth.

Fraser realised that he had got the answer to one of his questions; so he moved to the next.

"Have your cubs really got a skull?"

"What's that got to do with you?"

"Nothing really. I'm just curious. Is it a human skull?"

"They didn't kill anybody. They just found it. There wasn't even any meat on it. It was as dry as a stone on a hillside."

"Look," said Fraser patiently, "I'm not a gamekeeper. I haven't got a dog or the tame lightning with me; I'm not going to set any traps. Have you ever met a human who talked to you like this?"

"No," admitted Sionnaidh.

"Then why won't you trust me?"

"What do you really want?" she repeated.

"I just want to know where you got the skull. And there was another thing, a sort of coiled thing that was hard and shiny. You couldn't eat it; you'd have broken your teeth."

"My son found the skull up there," she jerked her nose in the direction of the boulders. "Under the stones. I don't know anything about the coiled thing."

"Thank you very much," said Fraser politely. He got to his feet. "I'll go and have a look round. By the way, if you're looking for rabbits a good place to go just now is… " and he gave her directions to a newly dug warren with young in it that Nephesh had told him about. "Good luck."

This information seemed to convince Sionnaidh of Fraser's good intentions for she relaxed her fighting position and when Fraser turned towards the boulders she trotted off to round up her cubs.

When she was at a safe distance she called back, "The skull's in the bracken over there. But there's really no eating on it."

Fraser picked it up.

It wasn't as big as he had thought a human skull would be, and the lower jaw was missing. Sandy had said it smelled bad, but Fraser thought that it was bare and clean and dry with no nasty smell such as he had imagined a dead skull would have.

"Of course Sandy has very bad taste," he said to himself. Just think of the things he thinks smell nice.

THE PIT

The hole through which the oldest of the cubs had pulled the skull was much too small for Fraser to crawl through. So he walked round the heap of stones looking for some other way in. On the south-east side, facing the point where the sun rises at mid winter, he found two huge upright stone slabs half buried in rubble, like doorposts, and resting on top of them an enormous boulder which, he thought, must have weighed tons.

There was very little space between this capstone and the debris that filled the doorway, so Fraser began to pull away the looser stones and clumps of heather to make a space big enough for him to get through. It was a slow business and soon his hands were bruised and bleeding. Worse still it was getting late and he knew he would soon be missed from home. But he knew that he was on the track of something; so he pulled and heaved until he had made an opening into which he could just crawl – hands out in front, body wriggling like a snake after them and legs pulled through last of all.

Then he was inside, on a rough floor of earth, under a roof of stone slabs which had partly collapsed so that they were tilted at crazy angles and there was barely room between them and the floor for him to crawl.

It was almost dark with the light coming from behind him from the entrance he had made. He wriggled forwards, stopping every few moments to get his breath back and hoping his tumblings of the mind wouldn't come back when he was in such a tight spot.

Then he found it in a pit a foot deep and as long as a dead body – a headless skeleton.

He moved a little to one side to let in more light. Did the bones move too?

"Rubbish," he told himself. "Just imagination."

Then, as his eyes grew more used to the light he saw something gleaming.

"Gold!" he gasped; everywhere there was the glint of gold. Little round discs, like pieces of a collar round the neck where the skull should have been; rings and bracelets and amulets on the hands and arms. Hardly believing what he was seeing Fraser stretched out a hand towards one of the bracelets to see if it was real.

At once there was a hiss, "Sstay."

Then he made his mistake; he snatched his hand away quickly; but not quickly enough. A flat head flashed like a dart, teeth like fine needles pricked the back of his hand and he felt the warm, sticky sensation of blood oozing over his skin.

* * *

Seti the adder had only wakened from her winter sleep in the warmth of that afternoon. She was still drowsy and, being deaf like all snakes, had not been aware of Fraser's approach until his white hand had stretched out in the darkness towards her. She would have crawled away if she could, but she felt trapped and struck instinctively, the poison flowing from her fangs.

"Sstay," she repeated. "Ssoon you will ssleep."

Fraser had never met an adder before, though he had heard about them and knew that their poisonous bite, which would kill a mouse in thirty seconds, could make humans very ill and was sometimes fatal. But he was more surprised than frightened, for this was the first time a wild animal had ever hurt him.

"Why did you do that?" he exclaimed in the kind of accent he would have used towards frogs or toads.

Seti crouched back in the crevice in which she had been hibernating; it was her turn to be surprised.

"What are you?" she hissed.

"I'm a human boy, but I speak like you and I am a friend. Why did you strike?"

Seti rolled in her coils. "How was I to know? I have just wakened after my sleep through the Dead Time and I've never heard of a human with a snake's tongue. When you sleep as I do you have to be very careful. Now, if you had been a badger…"

Fraser knew that any animal can make a mistake and strike before it sees what it is striking at and he had heard of cases where they had apologised afterwards.

"But," he wondered, "how can a poisonous snake say, 'I'm sorry?'"

He looked at the small puncture marks on the back of his hand. "What have you done to me?"

"You will fall asleep. All those I touch become still. You will be like these bones." With a dart of her tongue she pointed to the skeleton in the pit. "What has been done cannot be undone."

"Did you kill *him*?" Fraser glanced at the skeleton in the pit.

"Not me. He fell asleep before my mother's mother was as small as a headless worm." She slithered quickly away among the gaps and hollows in the stones and Fraser was left alone with the venom in his veins.

"At least," he said to himself, "I'll get out of here with some of the gold before the poison gets to me. Rona will come and find me and Sandy will tell all the animals that I am dead."

He stretched out his bitten hand again and lifted a bracelet from the cold arm in the pit and placed it on his other wrist.

"That will be proof," he thought. "They can come and dig the rest out for themselves."

Getting out was more difficult than coming in. In that narrow space he couldn't turn round and crawling backwards is much more difficult than going forward. He pushed backwards with the palms of his hands on that clammy clay floor and lifted his body on knees and elbows, and as he worked he gasped the stale air of the tomb.

Then, as in the thunder storm, came the tumblings of his mind; crash, crash, crash like fireworks in that subterranean cell. Flick, flick, flick, flick – like the darting of an angry snake's head.

When he wakened it was cold and dark without the slightest glimmer of light from any direction. Where was he? Where was the way out? Then he remembered; trapped in a tomb with a headless skeleton whose gold he had stolen. A skeleton which had seemed to move when his shadow had flickered over it.

He had held its skull in his hands. What if the rest of the bones should rise to claim it back from him?

UNDER THE BOULDERS

The phone rang in the vet's consulting room. Rona answered it.

"Can I speak to Rona... this is Fraser's dad... He's gone missing, didn't come home last night... Any idea where he might be?"

"Yes, I think I know... Yes I'm sure it'll be all right to get off work... Pick me up here... We'll bring Sandy; he's more likely to be able to sniff him out."

* * *

The car shunted to a stop outside the vet surgery. Rona dashed out. Fraser's dad stopped once to pick up the dog; then drove as fast as possible up the Range Rover Track till he came to the place where it had been washed away in the previous year's flood. Then Rona led him and Fraser's mum along the Goat Trail to where Sandy had found the skull.

"A human skull and a gold ring were found round about here just recently," she said. "Fraser was most anxious to find out where they came from. I'm sure this is where he would come looking for them."

There was, of course, nothing at all for a human being to see or hear or smell.

"I'll let Sandy off the lead. He'll maybe pick up Fraser's scent."

At first the dog ran about in circles, not understanding why he had been brought there and much more interested in tell-tale scents of rabbits and mice mixed with the strong smell of the foxes. Then Rona began to encourage him to range further afield, though she herself had no idea where they should be looking.

"Find," she shouted and waved her arms in a gesture she often used when she had hidden a treat for the dog to search for. Off he went expecting to come across a hidden dog-biscuit.

But then he stumbled on something much more interesting and stopped dead. In front of him was a hole in the rocks, flanked by an enormous stone slab on either side and with a massive capstone lying across the top. From inside the hole came a scent that he recognised. A terrier would have dived through the hole head first, but labradors are not used to going underground; besides there was another scent coming through which he did not understand, but which reminded him of toads and frogs. So he sat back on his haunches and barked.

Rona and Fraser's dad clambered over the rocks to join him and told him he was a good dog.

Sandy felt proud of himself and barked out his message as clearly as he could. "Fraser's in there; he may be hurt. But there could be something else there too that I don't understand, and I don't like it. What's the use," he thought. "They can't understand me."

This was only partly true for Rona understood enough about dogs to realise that Sandy had found something which might be worth investigating.

She turned to Fraser's dad, "There's something in there. Maybe it's him"

"Let's see," he said and crouched beside the opening. But it was far too small to let him in. "Can't get through that. Need to dig this lot away first."

"Perhaps I could get in," suggested Rona.

She put her head inside. "Phew! What a smell." Then she pushed her arms straight forward as if she was swimming and wriggled her body through the hole, easing her hips and legs in behind her. She landed on a flat, earthy surface.

"You all right?" called Fraser's dad from outside.

"OK *so* far, but there's not much space."

"Can you see anything?"

"It's pretty dark. Wait. There's something. Yes, it's him. Fraser! *Fraser!*"

"Is he all right?" Fraser's mum shouted from the Goat Trail below.

"I don't know. He's trying to say something. I can't make him out."

She shook the boy and he muttered something about gold and snakes.

"He's saying something about a golden snake. I don't know if he can move. I don't know how I'm going to get him out of here."

Fraser's dad hurled himself at the stones blocking the entrance, tearing at them with his bare hands till the nails broke and the knuckles bled. He had enlarged the opening by about a foot and sent several big boulders bounding down the slope onto the trail below when a sudden scream from his wife stopped him.

"No, stop! *Stop!*"

He followed her terrified gaze upwards and there was the massive capstone rocking like a logan stone as the whole structure below it shuddered and settled like a stag that has been shot collapsing in its death throes.

"They'll both be buried alive, "she screamed.

Fraser's dad watched in helpless horror as the ruin settled into a new position, but the door posts held and the entrance remained open.

In the pit Rona had a much less clear idea of what was happening, but she could hear the grinding of rock on rock as hundreds of tons of granite shifted above her.

"Rona!" Fraser's dad tried to make his voice sound matter of fact. "Can you hear me? You've got to be very careful. Take your time. Try not to knock against any of the stones. Do you think you'll be able to get Fraser out too?"

"I think so. He's conscious, but he's a bit confused and he's very tired."

Inch by inch she worked her way backwards; inch by inch she edged Fraser after her. Slowly the light from the entrance grew closer.

But at the least jarring of the rocks above Fraser's dad would shout, "*Stop!* Don't move." And the pair would lie, hardly daring to breathe, until the grinding stopped and they felt it safe to go on.

The most difficult part was actually getting back out through the entrance hole, for here it was almost impossible to avoid touching the unstable stones and the slightest pressure in the wrong direction would have brought the whole pile crushing down on top of them.

But at last they were out, flopping exhausted on the slope outside the entrance. And just in time. For, as if in anger at their escape, the great pile of boulders gave out a long, low growl and slowly crumpled before their eyes in a cloud of dust, blocking the entrance to the tomb forever.

Fraser couldn't stand without help and he was soaked in cold sweat. But he could talk; he babbled; he raved; he jabbered of gold and bones and snake bite, and he waved his right hand to show that it was bruised and swollen.

When Rona looked closely she saw on the back of that hand the marks of a bite and round the other wrist a bracelet of bright gold.

"I think he's been bitten by an adder," she gasped. "We'll have to get him to hospital."

THE SERUM

For days Fraser flickered between consciousness and unconsciousness in the hospital, vomiting and sweating, while his mum and dad sat at his bedside and tried to make sense of the weird, nightmarish hallucinations he seemed to be living through.

Before his eyes and in his dreams there passed a cavalcade of headless skeletons stretching out bony fingers to reclaim their stolen gold, snakes coiled in burrows guarding, with their venom, buried treasure and skulls staring accusingly and demanding decent burial.

But eventually the poison slipped out of his system, the sickness, the sweating and the dizziness passed and he became aware of the chatter of the starlings and sparrows on the ledge outside his window.

The consultant compared case notes with the doctor in charge of the ward.

"Most extraordinary case I've come across," he said. "The snake venom seems to have combined with the drug I was treating him with to attack the disease. If we can find a way of making a serum out of this we'll have a permanent cure."

Rona came to visit Fraser when he was able to sit up and talk.

"The gold," he said weakly. "There really was gold? I didn't dream it?"

"Yes," she said. "The people at the museum at Kilmore say that the bracelet you were wearing when we found you must have belonged to a prehistoric chief in the Bronze Age."

"So the skeleton and the snake, they were real too?"

"The museum people told me that the heap of stones you crawled under was the chief's grave. They found the skull; it's in the museum now."

"One-eye didn't come back?"

"I don't know anything about One-eye. You'll have to ask your animal friends about him."

But that was the one thing Fraser could not do for from the birds on the window ledge he heard only chirruping and chattering.

BETWEEN TWO
WORLDS

A DIFFICULT SUMMER

It was a difficult summer for Fraser. He had to attend hospital in Glasgow for endless tests; his tumblings of the mind came and went so that sometimes he was well and strong, but then he could not speak to his friends; at other times he was ill, feeble, dizzy and stumbling, but then he *could* talk to the animals.

When he was well he would go off with Jim Douglas, foraging around the farm and exploring the wood and the moor.

"Was it about here you found the skull?" Jim asked for perhaps the tenth time, for he had never quite given up the hope that he would find another skeleton and rob it of its treasure. But in the jungle of rocks and boulders on that stony hillside Fraser could never be sure exactly where the grave had been and, of course, the entrance was now blocked.

Then came the quarrel with Jim. His dad had given him an air rifle for his birthday and, as Fraser thought it was plain murder to shoot creatures he had once spoken with and befriended, that was the end of their friendship.

At the other times there was Sandy. Sandy was great fun and he delighted in showing Fraser things that Jim would never have spotted.

"A rabbit came along this way, not long ago."

"How do you know?"

"Easy. The scent's still fresh on the grass. Get down on all fours like me and have a sniff."

Fraser would crouch down, stick his nose into a patch of wet grass and snuffle as Sandy told him to, but he never could catch the slightest whiff of anything but damp earth.

"Just where your nose is now. That's it. Do you mean to say you really can't smell a thing? Maybe if your nose was wet like mine..."

Fraser would hopefully moisten the tip of his finger and rub his nose with it, but it made no difference.

"Well, if you can't smell anything, look closely; you can see where his feet have flattened the grass."

Fraser found that, with practice, he could see tell-tale signs which he would never have been able to detect without the dog's help.

Then they would make a game of it. Sandy would stop in the middle of a track through a field or in the wood and say, "Something's been here recently. What do you make of it?"

Sometimes Fraser wouldn't be able to see a thing and Sandy would jump about triumphantly because he was so much cleverer than the boy.

"A toad sat here for quite a long time and you really can't see the marks he left?"

"You're cheating," Fraser would reply. "You can't see anything either. You're using your nose to pick up the smell."

But quite often the boy would see the delicate mark of a bird's foot or the dried up silvery trail of a black slug and then they would both jump about happily to celebrate the pupil's progress.

Sandy was between two worlds, like Fraser himself. He spoke the same language as the wild animals and his senses of smell and hearing were as acute as theirs, but he didn't really understand them and as he invariably chased them whenever he got the chance, they never confided in him as they sometimes did in Fraser. Besides, he was never allowed out alone so that there was always a human following only a shout or whistle away to keep wild creatures at a distance.

There were often times, too, when Fraser was far too ill to go out with Sandy. During these periods his great delight was his conversations with Nephesh and Klamath who kept him up to date with all the interesting things that went on in the wild.

So after his quarrel with Jim, Fraser didn't know whether he wanted to be sick or well.

It was a difficult summer too for Bhuiridh. The deposed monarch had felt too ashamed to return to the herd as an ordinary subject at the court of the new king, so he had wandered off into exile, bitter and brooding, and worst of all lonely, for goats are sociable animals. Occasionally he met Fraser at the edge of the moor, but these had always been at times when the boy was well and could not talk to the animal.

Bhuiridh was not looking forward to the Dead Time ahead, alone, without company in the drizzle and sleet of winter, but the Autumn rut, when all the bucks were boasting and strutting and challenging was the worst time for a defeated champion to reappear.

* * *

It must have been difficult too for One-eye, if he was still alive. From time to time there were rumours, brought to Fraser by Klamath, of an old fox, sick and crippled, driven to eating slugs and beetles when he could not poach farmyard hens, skulking somewhere to the east beyond the moor.

"Bird gossip," Fraser thought and dismissed the reports, but when Klamath told him one day that the mighty Eye of the Wind himself had said that One-eye was hunting somewhere towards the moonrise beyond Sgurr Mor he felt that it must be true. Nephesh, however, still assured him that his old friend had never come back and that Feargal and Sionnaidh were hunting his territory.

* * *

It was also a difficult summer for Thorsa. In the green oasis of Bolstadur surrounded by the great lava desert of central Iceland the pinkfoot geese had discovered a perfect breeding ground where neither men nor arctic foxes could find them. Here she was hatched in the spring, the last from the egg, the smallest of the brood. As late as July she could not fly properly.

Then autumn, the shadow of winter, crept across the land. The low slant of the sun and the encroaching darkness warned the geese that the Dead Time would soon be upon them and they began to long for the lush water meadows of Islay and Dunadd.

When Ansar, the captain of the flotilla to which Thorsa belonged, saw the low sun at midday just fail to light up the white peak of Olafsfell to the north he knew that it was time to go.

Thorsa had to go too as skein after skein of geese took off in long wavering chains to escape from the darkness, the ice and the eerie northern lights. Although she did not realise it at first this was no flight to a neighbouring water meadow a few hundred yards away. It took her out over the tortured waste of lava and ashes and then across five hundred miles of unending ocean before the landmarks Ansar was looking for began to appear below – the white beaches of the Hebrides, the wicked saw-toothed ridge of the Black Cuillin on Skye – and he led the whole flotilla down in one breath-taking swoop on to the wetlands below Dunadd, by the side of the loch.

It was a journey Thorsa did not complete.

154

A TIME FOR DECISION

In the same week that Ansar decided to do something he had done year after year, seven hundred miles to the south in a medical laboratory in Glasgow, the consultant decided to do something nobody in the world had ever dared to do before; to inject deliberately a serum based on adders' venom into the veins of one of his patients as a last hope of curing his illness.

He was frank with Fraser's mum and dad. "There has been no time for proper clinical tests, but it's a gamble we have to take – and if it succeeds we may have a permanent cure. I have your permission?"

"There's no other hope?"

"None."

So Fraser went back to Glasgow.

Rona saw him off before starting work at the vet's surgery.

"That's Fraser away back to Glasgow to start a new course of treatment," she told Cathy. "He's going to be completely cured,"

Cathy said nothing.

"Isn't that good news?"

"Rona, this treatment Fraser's going to get, it's not a standard prescription you know."

"What do you mean?"

"It might not work as well as they hope."

"So he's not going to get better?"

"I didn't say that."

"What's going to happen to him? Is he going to die?"

Cathy had turned away; she was calling up the computer file on a pony they were going to visit on one of the farms that afternoon.

"I just said the treatment might not be as successful as you imagine. I don't think you should build up your hopes."

That afternoon they had to put the pony down.

Rona cried for the animal... and for Fraser.

* * *

Just two miles short of the wetlands by the loch where Ansar brought the geese down Thorsa fell behind the pace, lost height and clipped an electricity cable with one wing. Exhausted and in pain, she flopped down into a field of sheep belonging to Donald Douglas of Kilrasken. For a long time she crouched, as if sitting on a nest, her legs folded under her, and then at last she rose and waddled unsteadily across the field picking hungrily at the grass after her long flight across the sterile sea.

She had never seen sheep before. In Bolstadur there had been only geese and a few pairs of whooper swans. But the strange creatures kept out of her way; so she ignored them.

On the day after her landing, however, she met a new four-footed creature which seemed more threatening.

"Ho! Ho! Look what I've found," barked Sandy dancing round her in excitement.

"Keep away," she hissed stabbing at him with her long neck like a snake.

"I'm not scared of you," roared the dog, but he kept his distance, just out of range of that darting head. "If she'd run away I'd have a good chase," he thought, but with things that stand their ground and strike at you, you have to be careful.

"Stand off," she hissed again, striking furiously with her open bill but making no attempt to use her wings.

Then another creature appeared, not unlike herself, walking very slowly on two legs, but with wings that somehow didn't look much use for flying, and a voice she couldn't understand.

"Sandy! Come off! Come here!" shouted Rona. She clipped the dog's lead into his choke chain and hauled him away, boasting over his shoulder about the number of wildfowl he had eaten alive.

By the time she got home Rona realised that a single pinkfoot goose all alone who did not open her wings even when tormented by a dog must have something the matter with her. So she went back without Sandy.

Thorsa wasn't in the field, but she wasn't far away. She had clambered through a gap in the field wall and was waddling happily down the middle of the road from Kilrasken to Dunadd. She was not used to motor cars for there are no roads in Bolstadur.

When Rona approached she soon realised that the goose had an injured wing and could not fly. So she escorted her a long, slow mile into Dunadd, herded her into the compound at the rear of the vet surgery where calves and sheep were kept while they recovered after treatment, and shut her in, knowing that the high wooden fence would keep out predators and keep her in until she was able to fly again.

* * *

Thorsa was not the only refugee to look for a home in that field of Donald Douglas'. A few weeks after Rona had shepherded the goose away to safety, Bhuiridh arrived as the first sharp frosts nipped at night on the higher moorland.

157

Down he came, avoiding the rough ground where Gobhar would be holding court. He was looking for sheltered grazing and even more for company and in his old age a flock of black-faced ewes was not beneath him.

The ewes might have been impressed by his past reputation, might even have been glad to have him around, he thought, with a new pair of foxes on the territory, but they didn't show it. On the other hand they didn't object to his presence and so he might have found company and pleasant grazing for the winter.

Unfortunately, like Thorsa, he met a dog – Tess, killer of Kwarutta, and although he might still have stood his ground against the collie, when her master, Jim's dad, came up behind her bellowing challenges like a rutting stag and brandishing the tame lightning, he felt that there was no point in heroics and trotted back, butting through a hedge, onto the bleak, inhospitable moor.

BECOMING NORMAL

Fraser began his course of injections. There was a weekly routine: lie down; jag in the arm; "How do you feel? Glass of milk? You've got to lie still for twenty minutes now, you know."

Fraser was bored: bored waiting in hospital waiting rooms; waiting in hospital beds without his laptop or Xbox; waiting at home in Glasgow because he was not allowed out; waiting at night because he couldn't get to sleep; waiting by day because he had played all the games, visited all his virtual friends, and there was poor reception on his mobile.

Waiting to get better?

Waiting to forget his voices?

His only consolation was that he could still listen to the gossip of the garden birds:

"Ground's pretty hard today. Not much hope of picking anything up."

"I see the starlings are back. Little enough for the regulars without a crowd of them coming around."

"And the gulls. Why do they all have to come to our ground just when the feeding's at its worst?"

"Lady in the garden three trees away hung out a bag of nuts yesterday."

"No use to me. I can't hang upside down like a blue tit."

"I know. That's why I'm telling you."

"I sometimes wish I knew where the swallows go. They seem to have a wonderful place to visit in the Dead Time."

"You surely don't believe them? Making it all up, that lot."

Nearly all of this was trivial stuff and Fraser found that he missed his conversations with Klamath and Nephesh.

* * *

Cathy examined the lost goose.

"There's nothing seriously wrong with her," she announced. "Her flight feathers on one wing are damaged and she's pretty exhausted, but there are no bones broken."

"What'll we do with her?" Rona wondered.

"We'll keep her here over the winter and see how she does. Maybe by the spring she'll be able to fly off again."

In fact, Thorsa recovered quickly and soon became tame. She followed Rona round the compound and even made friends with Sandy.

"I think we've got a permanent lodger," said Rona one day.

"Well, if that's the case we'll have to see if one of the farms will take her. She can't stay here forever," said Cathy.

* * *

Fraser *did* get better. His tumblings of the mind became less common and much less violent. He first began to believe he might be on the way to recovery one morning when a large black-backed gull dropped into the garden. Gulls cover great distances and Fraser was looking forward to hearing any interesting news he might have, but when he tried to call to him the words refused to come.

Eventually he managed a "What moves?" so badly pronounced that the gull didn't understand him at first, and when it did reply he found he was only picking up the odd word and couldn't answer it properly.

Finally the gull gave up in disgust and flapped away.

"That's it," thought Fraser. "The voices are going." But that same afternoon he found to his surprise that he *was* able to conduct a perfectly intelligible conversation with a pair of jackdaws.

"What moves? How's the feeding?"

"Nothing much under the leaves," said one. "I've only had a couple of beakfuls of centipedes and beetles all day and I don't think I've had a single earwig."

"You've been looking in all the wrong places," said the other. "The lawn's soft enough to work on just now. I've had a few decent worms and there's spiders to be found if you know where to look for them."

"Where's that then?" asked the first innocently.

"That would be telling," said the other with a smirk.

Fraser was delighted that he had understood all this so well, especially as the jackdaws had used a lot of their own slang names for the creatures they ate.

Over the next few days the same thing happened several times.

One moment he would be unable to follow the gossip of street pigeons patrolling a car park; the next he would have no difficulty eavesdropping while a troop of starlings quarreled over some kitchen scraps, or he would be able to pick up the calls of rooks flying a hundred feet above his head.

Then the consultant came to see him specially.

"You're going to be all right now, you know."

"OK."

"You don't sound very enthusiastic."

"'S all right."

"Your treatment's nearly finished and you've responded well."

Fraser realised that he should be delighted – over the moon. He also knew that he should be grateful to the man who had cured him, and started to mumble some sort of thanks. But he also knew that, if the consultant was right, it was the end, this time forever, of his secret life in the company of wild birds and animals.

"Maybe I might not get really better?" he suggested.

"Of course you will," said the consultant, taken aback by his patient's lack of enthusiasm for being completely well again.

"When will I be better?" asked Fraser for the answer meant the limit of time left to him with his voices.

"You've another three injections still to get; then up to your holiday place at Dunadd for a week or two to get your strength back; then back to Glasgow to get on with your schooling. It's over now Fraser. You don't have to worry. You're going to be OK."

He shook hands with Fraser as if they had contributed jointly to some great triumph.

"How does it feel to know you're your old self again?"

"All right, I suppose."

"Is that all you've got to say?"

Fraser's thoughts were far away from that antiseptic-smelling Glasgow hospital. In his imagination he was in Dunadd with the resin-scent of the pines and the keen moor air in his nostrils; and in his ears the voices of the friends he might never again talk to.

"When I'm better," he asked, "will I be able to… " His voice trailed away as he realised that what he really wanted to ask could not be explained to this clever man.

"You'll be able to do everything you could do before," the consultant assured him. "You'll be absolutely back to normal."

Back to normal!

Back to being a dumb human; speechless in a country of a hundred tongues, deaf in a land of a thousand voices!

"Already it comes and goes," he thought. "I'm going to go back and talk and listen to them all again, before it goes for good."

THE WETLANDS

It was Easter and the weather, though still rainy and blustery, was a little less cold and raw than it had been.

Fraser persuaded his parents that, to help in his recovery, he should go up to the cottage between his weekly visits to the hospital for his injections. The consultant agreed and so Fraser found himself back at Dunadd again three years after that first spring when he had found he could talk to the birds and animals.

As the consultant had said that he should get as much fresh air and exercise as possible he had no difficulty getting away to roam the wood and moor. As he tramped about he felt all his old energy surging in his veins and muscles in a way he had not felt for three years, and this gave him a new calm confidence in himself.

He didn't tell Jim Douglas he was back and hoped he wouldn't meet him with his gun and his murderous bloodlust. He did tell Rona and explained to her why he had come; first he had to meet his friends for the last time; then he would come and visit her and Sandy and the new pet she had told him about, the pinkfoot goose.

Nephesh still came to the garden, but the neighbours had arranged a festoon of netting over the goldfish pool which Klamath found impossible to penetrate; so he did not come. Still, Fraser gradually got up to date with the best part of six months' news:

One-eye had still not returned a year and a half after his disappearance. Bhuiridh, too, had been wandering for nearly a year; he had been seen several times around Kilrasken, but Jim's dad had chased him away. Nephesh said he had tried to join the red deer during the winter when they came down to more sheltered country, but now that they had returned to the high moorland he was not able to keep up with them and was now grazing, lonely and sadly in the wood where he would be unlikely to meet the triumphant Gobhar. Fraser needed to see for himself; so he planned his expeditions carefully.

His first visit was to Klamath down in the wetlands by the loch side. He followed the Ballagan Burn through the wood where the traces of the great fire of a year and a half ago were gradually disappearing under a second spring's growth. There was Sebek's pool, black and brooding with a pair of moorhens dipping about at one edge. As he could see nothing in the depths he lay down on one elbow on the bank and listened.

There was no sound.

"What moves?" he called.

There was no reply.

He pulled a tuft of grass with a little mud still sticking to it and threw it on the water. As it drifted across the surface he could see the metallic glint of scales as the big fish rose slowly to investigate.

"I said 'What moves?' Didn't you hear me?" Fraser repeated.

"I move; I alone in the pool." That voice! That horrible grating voice. The pike saw there was nothing to eat and sank out of sight again.

"That's not what I came back for," said Fraser to himself. "I don't care if I never speak to *him* again."

He moved down stream out of the wood, past the lowest of the burn's waterfalls and on to the wetlands. He had never been as far as this before. From a distance it looked like a bright green field mottled by tufts of rushes and bog cotton. But the appearance was deceptive for the ground was sodden everywhere and the brightest patches of green hid places where there was no solid surface at all and the marsh plants floated on a bottomless sponge of ooze.

At first Fraser tried to pick a path through this quaking marsh, tiptoeing from tussock to tussock, trying to keep his feet dry, but after he had gone flat-footed into the soft green stuff several times he gave up and splashed straight on, accepting that there would be a row when he got home over the state of his socks and trainers.

The marsh was dotted with dozens of pinkfoot geese hungrily picking at the new green growth, building up their strength for the return flight to their summer breeding grounds, which, from the height of the sun, they knew they must soon make. They honked noisily at his approach, necks outstretched towards him.

"What moves?" he called.

"The sun, the height of the sun," said one.

"What do you mean?"

"When the sun first rises to the north of Sgurr Mor we will return to our home," hooted Ansar, the leader of the flotilla, already homesick for Bolstadur.

"Your home? Aren't you at home here?"

"For a time, yes, when darkness and ice close down over the north. But when the sun returns we long for the safest breeding grounds of all, where we can build our nests and hatch our eggs in peace, where the sun never sets and only creatures who can fly can reach us. Think of that, boy with a bird's tongue, no foxes, no dogs and none of your kind."

Ansar became excited at the thought and started hopping from one big webbed foot to the other honking, "The sun; the sun."

The others took up the cry and soon the whole flock was prancing about chanting, "The sun; the sun."

Fraser left them at it and moved on with soaking feet to where the burn flattens out before finally ploughing into the loch and there he saw Klamath fishing for eels in the shallows.

"Klamath, what moves?"

"Where have you been?" asked the heron.

"I migrated." It was the only way to answer the question, and not entirely untrue.

"This lot'll soon be off again. Time too. Noisy crowd."

"What's been happening?"

"Not a bad season for eels. Still a bit too early for frogs, but I see there's quite a bit of spawn about."

"What news on land?"

"Bhuiridh the goat, he's still wandering around like a lost hatchling on the moor. I hear the foxes have had another litter too."

"One-eye?"

"I hear stories from Eye of the Wind. You should really go up to the moor and ask him yourself."

And that was what Fraser decided to do next.

ON THE MOOR

It was a week before he could carry out his plan. First he had to go back to Glasgow for his injection, the second last of his course. Then his voices left him again and he wondered if, this time, they would come back at all.

However, they did and so he set off one blustery day to go up to the moor. He couldn't entirely avoid the traces of the great fire as he followed the Ballagan Burn past Kwarutta's pool. He climbed the steep slope past the rusting wreckage of Dyer's caravan on to the Goat Trail and then cut across the moor above it until he was at the foot of the jutting black cliffs of the Sgurr. He sat down on a boulder and waited.

Eventually in the distance there appeared a speck which Fraser could scarcely see. But that speck could not only see him, but recognised him as the "birdboy", to whom he had spoken before and about whose adventures he had heard from Klamath. So Eye of the Wind decided to find out what it was that brought the strange boy onto his territory and the speck grew into a pair of big, blunt, fingertip wings which dropped lower and lower in wide swinging circles until the eagle landed on a rock.

"Why have you come here?"

Fraser shuddered at the harsh steely voice and the sight of those vicious, hooked, blue-black talons. No wonder the hare and grouse were so terrified of Eye of the Wind.

"I want your advice. You see everything." Fraser started off with a little flattery, which worked with most animals, but the bird cut him short as it had the last time they had met.

"What do you want to know?"

"One-eye, the old fox, have you seen him?"

"I do not hunt crippled foxes."

"But you might just have seen him somewhere."

"Somewhere under the sun I may have glimpsed a fox, old and crippled, who is ashamed to show himself in better hunting grounds because he cannot face younger rivals. If he is still alive he might be your One-eye. But that was some time ago."

"Where is he?"

"Do you see that cloud?"

"Yes."

"Where will it be tomorrow? Your fox – if he is still alive – is now a wanderer without a home. Is that all?" The eagle opened his wings and launched himself into the air. In seconds he was again a speck, circling, always circling, and Fraser knew that when next he dropped, it would be to sink those talons into the flanks of a hare or the back of a grouse.

He shuddered again at the thought and looked in the other direction. There, below him on the Goat Trail, the herd was browsing by the edge of the wood. The powerful young buck standing on a rock on his own must be Gobhar. There was an older billy goat there too with one of his horns broken off at the tip and Fraser realised that Bhuiridh had at last swallowed his pride and rejoined the herd.

He trudged slowly across the moor. Perhaps One-eye too – if he was still alive – and then, somehow, he was certain that, although he would never be able to talk to him again, sooner or later, some windy night he would feel the thrust of a wet nose into his palm, the ruffle of silken ears under his fingers; and then there would be a bounding away into blackness.

EACH TO HIS OWN

Barook was more difficult to find than Klamath or Eye of the Wind. The badger never strayed from his sett until after dark and that meant a midnight expedition for Fraser.

He waited by his open bedroom window till a signal from Nephesh told him that Barook was out and about.

"Tell Barook I'll meet him where the rabbit track crosses One-eye's old trail."

"I will tell him."

Then he tiptoed downstairs, turning the key in the lock so carefully and closing the door behind him so gently that neither his mum nor dad heard. Then came the quick rush out across the garden and the walk along the trail he could have followed blindfold.

Barook was waiting.

"What moves?"

"I still move, a bit more slowly than I once did. More frogs and slugs and not as many young mice as when I was a cub."

"One-eye?"

"Never been back. You know a new fox has taken over the territory. He came here about a year ago, but I chased him off. I'm getting too old to put up with litters of fox cubs. He found himself an earth on the other side of the wood."

"Barook, I won't be able to come here again like this. You know I'm the only human who can speak your language."

"I have heard of others," said the badger, "but not in living memory."

"It comes to me sometimes," continued Fraser, "but at

other times I can't talk to you and I can't understand you and I can't explain how it happens. Now they are doing something to me that will make me only able to talk to other humans. It's nearly finished and so, after tonight, I won't be able to speak to you again."

For a long time the badger said nothing and Fraser wondered if he had fallen asleep.

At last he grunted, "That's how it should be. The badger lairs with the badger and the fox with the fox. In the spring the geese go back to their homes. The place of men is in houses behind doors barred and bolted like traps, not free with us in the woods. Go back to your own people."

Fraser turned away in tears and Barook vanished into the night.

* * *

"She's as tame as a farmyard goose," Rona told visitors to the surgery when they asked about Thorsa. "We'll soon have to find a farm to take her in."

But when April came and the first long skeins straggled overhead, northwards from Islay on their way to the arctic, Thorsa became restless and started calling to the wild birds in the sky. Her wing had long ago healed, but she had made no attempt to fly since she first arrived in the compound.

Then one day she was gone.

That night she came back to the compound. The next day she was off again and again returned at night. For a week she was away every other day, but always back in the evening.

Then one morning she took off after a wild skein and did not return that night – or ever again.

"She'll be somewhere in Iceland or Greenland," Cathy assured Rona, "with a mate and a nest and a clutch of eggs to hatch; and that's how it should be."

A NEW VOICE

Barook was the last beast Fraser spoke to.

The next day he travelled back to Glasgow for his final injection. Shortly afterwards he realised that he had finally lost his special voice, but had found another.

He was walking the old trail in the woods. There were birds galore: rooks, jackdaws, pigeons; and slow worms under leaves, and toads under stones, and fish and frogs in the burn. He heard their chatter only as jangles.

Then he heard another sound ahead on the trail; a crude stamping sound that seemed to come from somebody who did not care if all the woodland knew he was there, and he was face to face with Jim Douglas – with an air rifle under his arm and a cigarette in his mouth.

"Fraser, how you doing, mate?"

"Did you have to bring that thing?"

"Sport mate. Get a bead on them, steady, then bang!" He dragged on his cigarette and spat, "Anyway they're all vermin."

"Wood pigeons?"

"They're all the same. Look, we're farmers. You don't understand. They eat us out of house and home."

"Wood pigeons do that?"

"Aye."

There was a sudden flutter in the branches above them. Jim swivelled, swung his gun and fired. There was a harmless 'ping' as the slug stung through the branches and a pigeon fluttered away unhurt.

"Don't try that again."

"How not?"

"I'm telling you."

Jim laughed, broke the gun and reloaded with deliberate, exaggerated, insulting movements. He swung the barrel in a big arc.

A rook exploded from high in a treetop, "*Caw! Caw! Caw!*," was all Fraser heard.

Jim fired, but at the same instant Fraser struck the barrel of the gun upwards and the pellet flew wildly at the clouds.

"What the hell are you playing at?"

"I told you – don't try that again."

"You gonnae make me?"

"You better believe it."

"OK." Jim put the gun down and crunched his cigarette under his heel. "Come on."

They eyed each other like gunmen in a video.

Suddenly they grappled, like crabs, clutching each other and levering sideways, broke away and flung fists, clashed heads and backed off with bloody noses.

"Had enough?" challenged Jim.

"I'm waiting for you," Fraser's voice was strangely quiet.

Suddenly Jim realised, like Rona with Gobhar standing stubbornly in front of her, that there is a time to let well alone.

He picked up his gun. "Sod off! You don't own the place. I'll be back," and he turned away with what he hoped looked like a swagger.

Fraser stood his ground like a bulldog and only moved when he could tell by the tramplings and crashings that Jim was well out of the wood.

* * *

The next morning he wakened very early when it was still dark. He got up and opened his window. Nephesh had finished his hunting for the night and it was completely silent outside.

Then, like a signal, there was the whistle of a blackbird and within moments the still dark night was filled with the song of all the birds in all the woods and gardens of Argyll. Fraser watched as the sky slowly lightened until he could see the green of the lawn and the fields, and then, somehow, it was full, bright day. The music lasted a few minutes longer and then gradually faded.

His mum came into the room.

"Listening to the dawn chorus?' she asked. "Song birds sound so beautiful, just like the sound of flutes."

IF ONLY SHE KNEW!